Praise for

"I was completely consumed by this book. It was full of adventure, heartbreak, mystery and love." – Amy, Goodreads

"*Part of the Sky* completely blew me away. Intense. Creative. Highly recommended." – Denise, Goodreads

Praise for the SKY series

"5 MILLION STARS!!!!! … My new all-time favorite [series] ... Heart-stopping ... Jaw-dropping ... You need to read these books." – Megan, i fall in love book blog

"Every time I thought I had figured something out, the story took yet another twist and I was left re-thinking everything I had come to believe! ... This is a series that I will definitely be re-reading ... I cannot recommend it enough!" – Ashleigh, Goodreads

"AMAZING is such an inadequate description of this series ... It teaches you how to breathe all over again." – Tiffany, Goodreads

PART OF THE SKY

J.W. LYNNE

To Amy, Ashleigh, Debbie, Denise, Doug, Erica, Hanna, Lois, Lynn, Margery, Mark, Megan, Peter, Sally, Sara, Shannon, Sharon, Stephanie, Tiffany, and all those who returned to the sky with Seven and Ten … and wanted to know what happened next.

* * * *

PART OF THE SKY

MONDAY, JUNE 27
0527

SEVEN

I startle awake. The room is dark, but I can see well enough to tell that I am in my quarters at the warrior compound. Ten's undressed body lies next to mine. His breathing is soft and regular. I comfort myself by matching my breathing to his. *Everyone you love is safe, Seven*, I tell myself with each breath. *They're all safe.* But I'm not sure if I will ever believe that.

Under the spell of sleep, Ten appears completely at peace. His dark hair is wonderfully mussed and his lips are parted. I press my ear to his chest and listen to the steady beat of his heart. A heartbeat that, just nine months ago—when I left him to undertake a mission to save our baby—I thought I might never hear again.

That mission was an unqualified success. Our baby girl is now secure in the box under the ground, along with my family and Ten's family. They're all out of harm's way.

By all accounts, Ten and I are too. Even though the box that we occupy is above the ground, where there are Outsiders, it is well protected. And after the Outsider attacks nine months ago, the protection we are afforded here is certainly greater than ever before.

Suddenly, a piercing siren rips through the air. Ten grips me as he jolts awake.

"All personnel report immediately to the nearest airlock," a monotone female voice says through the communication system. Based on her tone, she could be announcing a meal, or a social event, or the time of day. There is no emotion behind her words to indicate the seriousness or lack thereof of her statement. I have a feeling though, that whatever is going on is extremely serious. As far as I know—at least since Ten and I have been here—there's never been an alarm like this before.

"What's going on?" Ten asks me, shifting himself into alertness.

"I don't know." And I'm not sure that I want to know. I'm not ready for anything other than a quiet first day back at the warrior compound. Morning physical training. Attending classes. Sharing meals with my fellow warriors. Perhaps a movie in the evening. But already today is proving to be far from ordinary.

I long to ignore the alarm. To plug my ears, wrap myself in Ten's embrace, and go back to sleep. But we have been given an order, one that I'm certain we are required to follow. Ten and I can't risk any extra attention or scrutiny right now, and so we pull on our jumpsuits, and we head to the hallway.

MONDAY, JUNE 27
0531

TEN

Just hours ago, Seven was given back to me, whole and complete. I'm not prepared for anything to go wrong yet, but it appears that something has.

As the disconcerting alarm blares, Seven scans open the door to her quarters. I release her hand, not because I want to, but because I don't wish to put us at any undue risk. Everyone who knows us probably assumes that we touch. Unlike back home—in the underground box where we lived our first eighteen years—touch is allowed here, but although we've never been told so, I get the feeling that it should be limited while in public. And so Seven and I keep most of our touches to our private moments alone in our quarters.

In the hallway, we are joined by our classmates. Everyone's hair is loose and unbrushed, but their jumpsuits are straight and neat and zipped all the way to the collar.

There is no conversation among us. Just quiet looks between us that say something isn't right.

Twenty-two catches my eye. I suppose he's eager to know how things went with "Murphy" on our first night back together in nine months. Even though he's one of my best friends, Twenty-two has no idea that the girl he calls Murphy is Seven rather than her twin sister, Six. He does know, though, how much I care for her. How much it hurt when she went away—although he doesn't know why she had to go. He certainly knows how grateful I am to have her back. He gives me a quick, uncertain look and then turns in the direction of the airlock. As I follow him, Seven by my side, Twelve nearly collides with the both of us.

MONDAY, JUNE 27
0535

SEVEN

"Watch it!" Twelve says, spinning toward us. His gaze flips from Ten to me and back again. Based on our direction of travel, he must deduce that Ten and I have come from my domicile.

Twelve scowls and looks away. He seems to be done engaging with us for now, which is good because I'm not sure yet how to deal with him. Ten said that, while I was gone, Twelve told everyone that he loved me. He also told Ten, in private, that he knew my true identity—that he knew I was Seven, not Six. That he knew Six and I switched places so I could be a warrior and Six could stay in our box back home. He didn't say how he knew, and it is possible that he said it purely to unnerve Ten, without actually believing it to be true. But if that switch is discovered, anyone who knew of it is in grave danger. And so we must keep Twelve on our side.

I'm fairly certain that Twelve doesn't *actually* love me. From the time we were very young, he has been nothing but cruel to me. I suppose cruelty could be the result of love marred by jealousy. Ten and I were inseparable from the time we were toddlers, best friends always. Could that explain Twelve's nastiness? Was he acting out because he was envious of my close bond with Ten?

What would I have done if Ten had been paired with someone other than me on Assignment Day and he was forced to mate and raise children with her? Or worse, what if he had fallen in love with someone else in our preschool classroom long ago? The thought makes my chest ache with the desire to embrace Ten, right here in the hallway. *I can't imagine not being Ten's best friend.*

But if Ten loved someone other than me, I would never be cruel to him, never taunt or tease or humiliate him. I would never, ever hurt him, no matter how much he hurt me.

I stay beside Ten as we move through hallways patrolled by black-jumpsuited soldiers who hold large, powerful-looking weapons at the ready. Whatever is going on, it is clear now that it is serious.

Soldiers order people into the airlock, crowding us inside so tightly that our bodies touch one another. I am reminded of how, as brand-new warriors, my classmates and I were packed together in an elevator for our first journey up here. Unlike back then, the bodies that contact me now are tense, but not trembling. We have learned to control our fear. At least to a point. We've learned not to let on when we're afraid. To never let our fear show.

No matter what.

MONDAY, JUNE 27
0538

JACKIE

My heart races as I join other soldiers on a march
toward the nearest airlock. An evacuation alarm before
morning reveille on the first day that Murphy fully rejoined
us makes me uneasy. Although she seems not to remember
it now, somewhere deep in her brain, Murphy knows—or
once knew—my deepest secret. From now on, I will live in
fear of her.

Part of me regrets that I put myself in a position to fear
her. I didn't have to tell Murphy my secret. I didn't have to
tell her that I am "the enemy." I didn't have to give her
Jose's rook, but I made a promise to him, and after he kept
his promise to me—almost losing his life in the process—I
felt I owed him. Still, it was unwise.

Hopefully, Murphy will never recall that I told her my
secret. Her memory was wiped after I did so. Jose's rook,
which mysteriously disappeared during her time at the

hospital, should hold absolutely no meaning for her now. I shouldn't be concerned. My secret is secure in the forgotten parts of her mind.

As I enter the airlock, I maintain complete silence. I hold my body the way I have been taught and behave exactly as I am expected to. If today's alarm is due to an actual emergency, deviations from expectations will likely be tolerated, because those who enforce the rules will be preoccupied. But if this is only a drill, any deviation from the rules will be swiftly punished. Unlike back home—with the Outsiders—discipline here is severe.

At times, it is deadly.

MONDAY, JUNE 27
0541

TEN

The outside door to the airlock opens and a cool salty breeze, along with the sound of crashing ocean waves, invades the oppressive stillness of the air around us. Faint daylight is visible above the faraway mountains of rock that mark the end of the beach, but the sky over the ocean is still dark. Lighted drones hover above us in the air, providing some minimal illumination.

We proceed down the gleaming silver ramp and onto the sand. As soldiers scan our left forearms with a handheld device, I stare at the shiny black buildings of the warrior compound that seem to float above the ocean. They look rather menacing in the dim light. Like they hold dangerous secrets. Perhaps they do.

After we are scanned, we are sent to join some of the instructors. I am reassured to see Ryan among them. He glances distractedly in our direction.

11

"Have a seat on the sand," he says, more to Seven than to me. "We might be here a while." His tone is easy and relaxed, but his forehead is creased with tension. I wonder if he knows what's going on. I try to ask that question without words, but he nods me away. At the same time he whispers, "Stay close."

MONDAY, JUNE 27
0543

JACKIE

The beach is swarming with people. At least five hundred of them. It appears that nearly everyone is now evacuated from the compound. I get my arm scanned and I'm sent to muster with the other soldiers in my duty group. No one talks. No one breaks rank. Our eyes scan for danger, from above, from the cliffs, from the compound, from the ocean. We still have no idea of the threat we face, or whether there is any threat at all.

I feel it deep in my gut before I become fully aware of what is happening. Six soldiers converge on one. Their target is a man. I know him. I've known him my entire life. Ray Miller. That was his birth name. Here he goes by David Erikson. He is like me—an Outsider hiding in the military in plain sight.

I want to call out to Ray. A warning. But no matter what I do now, his fate is already sealed. I watch, powerless, as he is slammed face first onto the sand. His blood spatters the ground. Ray struggles, unwilling to give up despite the fact that he is hopelessly outnumbered.

A moment later, he goes limp. Probably not dead, but as good as dead. If he is not sentenced to a quick execution, he will wish he was. Whatever crime he is suspected of committing, it must be egregious if his arrest required this type of event.

Did they discover that Ray is an Outsider? If so, do they think there are more of us here? Was his public arrest meant as a message to us, a threat?

As Ray's inert body is dragged away, pain and guilt wrack my soul, making it difficult to remain quiet and still. As much as I mourn the loss of my friend, a boy who once taught me to ride a bicycle when no one else would, I can't help feeling grateful that it isn't me whose time here is up. But that relief is small, because I now see firsthand how much I am in danger. Ray is gone. I could be next.

MONDAY, JUNE 27
0553

SEVEN

The man's boots slide across the sand, leaving two faint streaks that mark his path. Who is that man? Why did the soldiers attack him? What was his offense? I slip one hand between Ten and me, so that our fingers touch. Touching him brings some comfort, but of course it doesn't bring the answers that I urgently seek.

A loud burst—like the earlier sirens, except short and quick—sounds twice. "All clear. Please return to your scheduled activities. All clear," a male voice says without emotion. The threat has apparently been neutralized. But I have no idea what threat was posed. Or whether the man who has just been pulled inside a waiting terrestrial drone was even a threat at all.

Ryan is alternately watching the drone and scanning the crowd. What does he know? Does he think there is still danger? Of course there is still danger. There will always be danger here. It is naïve to think otherwise.

The small aerial drones above our heads extinguish their lights and silently speed back toward the warrior compound. Their illumination is unnecessary now that the sky has gone from blue-black to pink with puffy clouds.

Ten and I stay close to Ryan as we trek back over the soft sand and up the ramp that leads into the airlock. As the door begins to close behind us, Twelve slips into the already packed space. He catches my gaze. His eyes are hard and cold. The same way they've been for as long as I can remember. Although I want to look away, I don't. I need to be strong, the way Ma'am taught me to face threats.

Twelve holds my gaze as if he controls it. The same way he always has. But I keep my eyes locked with his long enough that he breaks his stare before I do. It may be a victory, but only a small and temporary one. I don't dare celebrate it, because celebration brings distraction and I must not allow my attention to be diverted.

There are many threats up here, both the known and the unknown. Maybe if I had never felt danger I would feel safe here, but I know what it's like to be attacked, to have my sense of security shattered. It has happened before and it could happen again at any time. Without provocation. Without warning.

I am not safe.

And I never will be.

MONDAY, JUNE 27
0600

SIX

I snap into consciousness. It's time to feed Fifty-two. My navigator alarm has sounded, the way it has every three hours since I returned home. This time was different though, because I was in the middle of a vivid dream.

I was back in The White Room at the Outsider's compound. Ryan wasn't there with me. I didn't know how long he'd been gone or who had taken him, but somehow I felt certain that he wasn't coming back. I was in a panic, crying and screaming, "Ryan! Ryan! Ryan!"

Slowly, the door began to creak open. I tried desperately to catch my breath and ready myself for whoever was on the other side.

And then Jose stepped into the room. I felt a bit of relief, but worry rapidly overtook it.

"Where's Ryan?" I asked him.

Without a word, Jose shut the door behind him and

walked over to me. He sat beside me on my mattress, much closer than I'd expected him to, sending my heart pounding again, but this time, instead of panic, I felt my skin prickle with anticipation, and maybe excitement. He leaned toward my ear, his breath warming my cheek. "Ryan's fine. They'll be bringing him back soon. I'm going to stay with you until then. Okay?"

"Okay," I breathed, feeling reassured. Somehow, despite my earlier certainty that Ryan would never return, I knew Jose was telling me the truth.

And then Jose's fingers touched my chin, and ever so gently turned my face toward his. He looked deep into my eyes as his hands embraced my shoulders. I grasped his upper arms, feeling the strength of his muscles. That strength made me feel so safe.

Our clothes seemed to melt off, without anyone's effort to remove them. Jose pressed his naked body against mine, and wonderful heat coursed through me, settling in the center of my chest. I held him tighter as his body pushed against me over and over, joining itself with mine. Mating with me.

Then I woke up.

I shake the disconcerting dream from my consciousness, pushing it far enough away that I no longer feel the heat it kindled inside me. Then I take a warm bottle of formula from the cabinet. I lift Fifty-two into my arms and slip the sipper of the bottle between her lips. Without opening her eyes, she begins to feed calmly, peacefully.

I can't imagine how Seven was able to entrust her precious daughter to me. I suppose she really didn't have much of a choice. I'm glad now that I never told her something I thought about often when I was younger. About how I never wanted to be a mother. I never wanted to be responsible for raising a child. I don't think I have the ability to nurture another person. To sense their feelings. To reassure them. To make them strong. I'm not even able to do that for myself.

Seven would have been a wonderful mother. She is remarkably selfless and generous. It always struck me as strange that we are identical genetically, but so different in our minds.

Of course, now that Fifty-two is mine, I will strive to be the best mother to her that I can be. Whatever I must do. Whatever it takes. I will protect Fifty-two's life at the expense of my own. The way Seven did for me.

MONDAY, JUNE 27
0605

TEN

Seven and I separate to shower and dress in the fresh jumpsuits that have been delivered to our quarters. With so much uncertainty going on, I hate to separate from her. Although she is strong enough to fend for herself, we are stronger together.

Even though we have only been apart for minutes, I feel myself exhale with relief when I see her sitting at our dining table. Her hair is secured in a perfect bun, looking as if she might have just arrived for morning class with Professor Adam. Part of me wishes I could return us both to that time. A time when I never wondered whether someone or something would take Seven from me. Back then, I never considered that I could lose her so easily, but here …

"So what do you think that soldier did to warrant an attack like that?" Twelve asks, breaking the relative quiet.

"I wish they'd tell us," Nineteen says, "so we don't

accidentally put ourselves at risk."

"Yeah," Twenty-two agrees. "We've been up here for over a year, and we still have no real understanding of how things operate. They tell us just enough to work on whatever problem we're trying to solve, but no more."

Just like back home, I think. From the look Seven gives me, I am certain she's thinking the same thing. I retrieve my breakfast tray and join my friends at the far end of the table. They each offer me a quick nod and then return their focus to their meals. As I take the first bite of mine, I realize how hungry I am. I haven't had much appetite for the past nine months. I've had to force myself to eat every meal, but now my appetite has returned with unrestrained vengeance.

Seven looks down at her navigator and sighs. She turns the screen so I can see it.

Report for rehabilitation at 0700.
Hospital Wing 6-0.

"What's wrong?" Thirteen asks her.

"They're sending me to rehab," Seven says.

"It's not so bad," Thirteen reassures her. "I went for a month after I recovered from my coma. I think they made me even stronger than I was before the accident."

Seven sighs and looks to me for a second opinion.

"There's nothing wrong with taking things slowly," I say.

Physically, Seven appears to be entirely back to normal. Her body, even completely undressed, looks indistinguishable from before she left, but she can't afford to risk injury. Seven needs to be at her very best right now.

We all do.

MONDAY, JUNE 27
0649

SEVEN

As I stand, Ten collects his tray. "Would you like me to walk to the hospital with you?" he asks me.

It would be comforting to have Ten accompany me to my first day of rehab, but I don't want him to be late for PT. I don't want to risk him—and our classmates—being punished for his tardiness. Now that our class is considered a team, a mistake by one leads to punishment of all.

"I'm fine." I brush Ten's hand with mine, sending a pleasant shiver through both of us. "I'll see you in class, Hanson."

"See you in class, Murphy," he says, keeping back a smile.

I drop my tray in the recycle chute and go toward the hospital, keeping my pace quick. Although I might be granted some leeway if I arrive late—after all, I was just discharged from the hospital yesterday and I am surely not expected to be completely back to my normal abilities—I don't risk it.

Two minutes before seven, I scan my arm at the door to Hospital Wing 6-0.

"Welcome, Murphy. Come on in," a female voice says through the communication system.

The door to the unit slides open and I enter a spacious room that is reminiscent of a gymnasium prepared for family recreation, with large colorful blocks and balls set out on padded mats. But the dozen or so people in this room are much too old for children's toys.

A woman with wavy blonde hair, which extends down only as far as her neck, walks toward me at a fast clip, faster than seems normal. She's human, but a bit intense. The red letters "PT" on her collar tell me that she's a physical therapist.

"Murphy, I'm Raquel Carter. I'm going to be your Rehabilitation Champion," she says.

Rehabilitation Champion? What a strange term for a physical therapist. I almost laugh, but I catch myself and cough out, "Nice to meet you, ma'am."

"You can skip the formalities," she says pleasantly. She leads me to an adult-sized purple pod with all kinds of wires and tubes protruding from it. "Please remove your jumpsuit and have a seat," she says.

Back home, I'd never be asked to undress with other

people in the room, but up here, things are different. It's going to take some time to readjust to the lack of modesty.

Obediently, I slip off my jumpsuit—leaving my underwear in place since Carter didn't ask me to remove it. Then I recline into the pod.

Carter quickly goes to work, attaching sticky wires to my arms, legs, and chest, and strapping some kind of oxygen mask over my face. Then I feel the pod grip me, taking hold of my body as if it is consuming me into itself.

"No need to be alarmed," Carter says to me. Rather than reading my thoughts or even my expression, she has probably noted a change in the data monitored by the myriad wires she has attached to me. I'm sure some of my vital signs are venturing into the red zone. Without waiting for me to relax, she continues, "I'm going to run you through some range of motion exercises to give me an idea of your baseline flexibility. Just relax your muscles and let the pod do the work for you."

For the next ten minutes, the pod takes nearly every one of my joints and flexes, extends, and occasionally rotates them in various directions. It feels strange to be manipulated like this, uncomfortable having my body move out of my volition. After the pod has assessed me, it turns me upright, depositing my feet onto a floor that is now a bit spongy.

Carter attaches a band to my waist. "Next, we're going

to assess your balance. As the floor shifts, try to remain standing upright, but don't worry, you won't fall. If you start to lose your footing the safety band will catch you."

The floor tilts, right and left, front and back, sometimes shifting slowly, sometimes suddenly. I only lose my balance once, and I probably could have righted myself on my own if the safety band hadn't caught me first. Still, the exercise is more challenging than I feel like it should be, and the experience makes me feel weak. I guess the past few months have taken their toll on my body.

"You did very well," Carter says when we are through. Her statement makes me feel even weaker. She goes on, "The final part of the physical assessment is ambulation evaluation. I'd like you to begin walking forward. Try to match your pace to that of the moving walkway beneath your feet. Are you ready?"

"Yes," I say, taking a deep breath to gather my energy.

The floor starts moving—like a treadmill, but slowly, much slower than I'd ever walk in real life. I wish it would go faster. I try to urge the floor to move quicker with my steps and it seems to speed up in response.

"Don't try to outpace the walkway, just walk along with it," Carter says to me. I slow my pace as instructed and gradually, the walkway brings me up to a normal walking speed. "Excellent," Carter says. "Now we're going to try an easy jog. Do you feel ready for that?"

"Yes." I haven't jogged in months, and the thought makes me giddy.

The walkway begins to pick up speed and I begin to jog. Faster. Faster.

"Keep pace with the walkway," Carter reminds me.

I was going too fast. I slow down.

"Very good," Carter approves.

Gradually, the treadmill picks up speed. It gets fast enough that I have to run to keep pace with it, and so I do.

"Outstanding," Carter says. "You're doing very well."

The running feels good. Really good. My earlier weakness seems to have faded away. My muscles fill with desire. I want to go faster. As fast as I can. I want to run without restraint.

"Slow down," Carter says.

But I don't. My desire to run is irrepressible. I don't just *want* to run. I *need* to run. I need to release all the stress and uncertainty and pain and fear that has built up inside me. To rid my body of it.

"Murphy, slow down immediately!" Carter shouts.

I ignore her. I know I shouldn't, but—

Suddenly, the safety band around my waist goes painfully tight, many times tighter than it did earlier, when I nearly lost my balance. At the same time, searing pain grips my midsection. It feels as if I have been struck by a dozen weapon hits all at once. It is so overwhelming that everything within me goes limp.

As the safety band deposits me back into the purple pod, I wipe away my tears with hands that feel as if they've turned to rubber. "What happened?" I ask breathing hard.

Carter's gaze pierces into me. "I told you to slow down," she says coolly.

Icy fear prickles my tender, tingling skin. I'd thought maybe the machine had malfunctioned, but now I'm sure that Carter caused my pain on purpose. And she made no attempt to hide it from the others in the room. What she did to me must be acceptable for those who fail to follow instructions.

I would have expected punishment if this was part of my training, but Carter is my physical therapist. She is supposed to be helping me to heal. I didn't expect to be punished here. But I suppose I should have.

"I apologize," I say, averting my eyes from hers.

Until I am released from rehabilitation, I am at Carter's mercy.

I must listen to her every order. And, if I wish to avoid punishment, I must obey.

MONDAY, JUNE 27
0743

SIX

Infant Stim is where babies are cared for while their parents go about their workday activities. It is where I stayed when I was an infant, and where I must leave Fifty-two.

As I enter, a dark-haired female robot, Miss Jeanine, gives me a perfect broad smile and greets me, "Welcome to Infant Stim!" She holds out her right hand and I place my left forearm above it, allowing her to scan me. A moment later she continues, "How is our young Fifty-two this morning?"

"Very well, thank you," I say.

Her hand remains palm upright. I gently position Fifty-two's tiny arm over the robot's hand. Fifty-two doesn't struggle. She has done this many times before.

"Good morning, Fifty-two," the robot says in a higher-pitched sing-song voice.

Fifty-two humors her with a smile.

Miss Jeanine extends both arms toward the baby. I bite back my discomfort and hand Fifty-two to her. Fortunately, Fifty-two doesn't cry. It would be much harder to let her go if she did.

"We'll see you later, Mommy," the robot says to me.

I gently touch Fifty-two's forehead with the tips of my fingers, knowing that it is the last human touch she will have until I pick her up after work, then I nod at Miss Jeanine and, fighting everything inside me, I leave.

MONDAY, JUNE 27
0745

SEVEN

My muscles are just starting to regain their strength when the purple pod tilts upright and the "safety band" helps me to my feet.

"How are you feeling?" Carter asks as if she didn't just jolt the life out of me minutes ago.

"I'm fine," I say.

She presses a button and the wires detach from my skin, then she removes the mask from my face and the band from my waist. When she is through, she asks me to get dressed. I guess our therapy session is over. *Good.* I've had enough of Carter for today. I just want to go to class where I can see my friends and recover from rehab. I check the time on my navigator. 0747. It looks like I will have some time to collect myself before our first lecture of the day begins.

Carter stops at a door and turns to face it. My

shoulders tense. *This is not the exit to the rehab unit.* It looks like the entrance to an office of some kind, but the door is unmarked. I wonder if I will be taken inside to be lectured on the importance of following Carter's instructions during my physical therapy visits. Or perhaps I am to be punished further for my behavior this morning. Perhaps the painful shock Carter administered wasn't deemed adequate.

The door opens.

"I have Sarah Murphy," Carter says into the room.

A brown-haired woman with dark skin who sits behind a lone broad desk nods. "Come in, Murphy."

As soon as I step inside, the door closes behind me, leaving Carter outside. I'm glad to be free of her, but I don't relax, because what I'm about to face could be even worse.

"I'm Doctor Karen Johnson," the woman at the desk says. She gestures to a reclined blue pod opposite her desk. "Go ahead and lie down."

I don't trust pods anymore, but at least this one doesn't have any tubes or wires sticking out of it. I follow Doctor Johnson's instructions and lie down. The pod instantly conforms to my body, but it doesn't grip me like the purple one did. It gives my body what feels like a warm, gentle embrace.

"How are you feeling?" the doctor asks.

"All right," I say, wary. I can no longer see Doctor Johnson, but I am certain that, with the aid of a monitor of some sort, she can see me.

"I'm sure you're wondering why you have come to visit with me," the doctor says.

"Yes," I respond, eager to know what I'm facing.

"Individuals who have undergone induced retrograde amnesia—as you have over the past several weeks—often have questions or concerns," she says. "I'd like to talk with you about your feelings regarding the experience." And then it makes sense, why I have been brought here. Doctor Johnson must be a psychiatrist.

I've never visited a psychiatrist before. Back home, some people are assigned to be treated by that type of doctor after a friend or family member dies—especially if the death was unanticipated—or when a friend or family member is sent to isolation. Otherwise, visits to a psychiatrist are rare.

Doctor Johnson continues, "Yesterday, in the hospital, you told Doctor Simon that your last memory prior to the onset of your amnesia was of traveling in a terrestrial drone, returning from an outside compound. Sometimes, additional memories are recovered after the initial rebooting period. Have you remembered anything further?"

I take a moment to think about my response. The goal of the memory wipe was to erase all recollections of my captivity by the Outsiders. What the doctors don't know is that *I* was never captured by the Outsiders. The person who was held prisoner was Six, but then she and I switched identities. Her memory was only partially wiped of her experience, because I took her place for the last two weeks of the procedure. Fortunately, thanks to Ten's technical skills, none of my memories were lost. When I awoke in the hospital room, I knew I had important secrets to protect, but my mind was still clouded. In order to be certain to shield the fact that Six and I had switched places, twice, to protect my baby, I told Doctor Simon that I'd forgotten more than what she'd anticipated. Now I have the chance to change my answer, but I must be cautious about the one that I give.

If I tell Doctor Johnson that I don't recall anything further, she will probably fill me in on some of the important events that occurred between then and now. She will tell me that some of the people who I once knew are now dead. I will be forced to grieve all over again for the loss of my instructor, Ma'am. Tears burn my eyes.

"I remember that our drone was attacked. People died." My voice breaks. "My instructor died."

"Yes," Doctor Johnson says, her voice soft and gentle. "How did that make you feel?"

I take a shaky breath. "Hurt. Powerless. Angry …"

Perhaps it isn't a good idea to be so honest with this stranger.

"Those feelings are completely normal," the doctor says.

I swallow and compose myself. "That's how I remember feeling back then, but I feel better now," I say, trying to convince her that I am recovered, that I am well enough not to require her concern. "I still miss my instructor. I'm still angered that she was taken from us. But those feelings just make me want to do my job better. To be an exceptional warrior. In her memory. To do what would make her proud."

"That's a healthy way of looking at this," the doctor agrees.

I nod, satisfied that I've achieved my intention.

"Let's move on now to the very last thing you remember prior to your stay in the hospital," the doctor suggests. "What would that be?"

It's probably better if I pretend that my memories stop right before I found out I was pregnant with Fifty-two, that way I won't risk inadvertently exposing any secrets. "I remember Lieutenant Commander Ryan informing me of my instructor's death. I remember grieving," I say. "That's the last thing I recall." That was just before Ryan gave me the pregnancy test.

"Okay," the doctor replies. "Has anyone told you what happened after that?"

"No," I say, offering her yet another lie. "What

happened after that?"

I can almost hear the doctor considering her words before she finally speaks, "You were taken prisoner by the same enemy who attacked your terrestrial drone. Your body and mind were tortured severely. Fortunately, there will be no permanent ill effects. Your scars have been healed, and your mind has been protected by the medically-induced amnesia. It is best that you do not try to recall any of the memories that have been removed. To do so will cause you undue stress and possible lifelong sequelae. It is time to move on with your life. To do as you said: to be an exceptional warrior. Do you understand?"

"Yes," I say. But all I can think of is Six. My mind is filled with vague images of the torture she must have endured in the hands of the brutal Outsiders. I can't even begin to visualize what they did to her, but I can clearly see the pain they inflicted.

A surge of guilt constricts my gut. Six didn't get to complete her memory wipe because she had to switch places with me. She lost *some* of her memories, but not all. Now, she will have to live with whatever recollections the procedure didn't remove from her mind.

Six seemed remarkably composed when I last saw her, but that provides me with no reassurance. Internal trauma isn't always visible from the outside, especially if someone is skilled at hiding it. And Six is quite skilled. I think I'm the only person who she has ever allowed to see her in pain.

I hope she isn't suffering now. I hope Nine and Three and my family are somehow helping her move past her experience, even if she refuses to tell them anything at all about it. I hope she can find the strength to accept their help.

I hope she can find the strength to go on.

MONDAY, JUNE 27
0840

SIX

Today, I ate breakfast with my family. The conversation was very ordinary. For a few moments, I felt as if nothing had changed in the past nine and a half months. And yet everything has changed. At least for me.

I look at things differently now. The images on the walls of the dining room are no longer of places that exist only in the imagination. I have seen mountains just like the ones in the images, and rippled blue-green water that goes on forever. Above the sky the water undulates. In the images, the water is still, lifeless. There are also images here of things I didn't see during my time above the sky, but those things probably exist too. Why shouldn't they?

My friends and family seem different too. I notice feelings in them that I've never detected before. I see upset in my parents' eyes when they look at me. They are worried about me. I haven't told them about my experience and I don't think I ever will completely. It would distress them to know the danger I was in, and it would make them worry too much about Seven.

My little brother, Forty-one, seems awed by me. I think he wishes he could have gone above the sky too. He might be required to someday, if he is assigned to be a warrior. But as much as I think he would be an excellent warrior, I don't know how I would survive losing another sibling.

In the eyes of Nine, I see compassion. I have a feeling that it was always there, but I was too preoccupied to see it. Even though I've shared a domicile and a bedroom capsule with him for more than three months, I never really looked him in the eyes until recently.

Three and I haven't interacted much since my return. To be honest, I've been avoiding her. I'm still trying to figure out the thoughts and feelings in my brain. My mind is a bit confused about my time above the sky. And my dream last night only made things more difficult. I can't help feeling guilty, knowing that I might have mated with Jose. And worse, that I might have done it by choice rather than by obligation. Did I love Jose more than I love Three? Is that even possible?

What bothers me the most though is that, as much as I am grateful to be with my friends and family again, a small part of me wants to go back above the sky, even though the thought of it absolutely terrifies me. I yearn to see more of what's there. To ask Ryan to fill in my missing memories. Maybe to see Jose and try to figure out how I felt about him. But of course I would never really go back. Not of my own volition. Up There is extremely dangerous. I saw that firsthand.

As we get up to leave the dining room, Forty-one asks me to walk him to school. He hasn't done that since he turned eight years old—"a grown boy, fully capable of walking himself to school," he'd said. But now, after my return from Up There, perhaps he's feeling nostalgic.

Rather than go with my parents to our workplace, I turn toward the school with Forty-one. "We can't walk together the whole way," he says to me apologetically. "My friends would tease me."

I recall my own worries when I was a child, the desire to be like the other children. To not call attention to myself. To fit in. "It's not easy being nine years old," I say.

"I think life gets a little harder every year," he says.

"It does," I agree. "But you grow a little more ready for it."

"Is it easier being a grown up?" he asks, skimming the sleeve of my blue adult jumpsuit with that of his white children's one. Just over a year ago, I wore a white jumpsuit, and I had all the freedoms that come along with it. The freedom to make mistakes—as long as they were small ones. The freedom to play—at designated times and in designated areas. To explore—anyplace that wasn't forbidden. I never really appreciated those freedoms then. Now, I long for them.

"In some ways yes, and in some ways no," I answer.

He glances behind himself and then whispers, "Do you still have Seven's tag?"

Of course I do. I haven't let it out of my sight. I've kept it on its chain hanging around my neck ever since I used it to make my way back from the drone closet after Seven and I switched places for the last time.

Technically, the tag belongs to Forty-one. Ten gave it to Seven and Seven gave it to Forty-one the night before the first time she left for Up There. I don't think our parents would approve of Forty-one owning something so dangerous, but that isn't the reason I haven't returned it to him. There's something I want to do with it first.

"Do you mind if I keep it for a little while longer?" I ask Forty-one.

He looks at me, probably ready to respond with the obvious question, *Why do you want to keep it?* But he doesn't ask it. Maybe he senses that my answer is too private to share. Sometimes it amazes me how perceptive he is for someone so young. Then again, children are more perceptive than adults in some ways.

"Keep it as long as you need," he says.

"Thanks, little bro," I say. I haven't called him that in a while. We used to refer to each other as "little bro" and "big sis" when we were younger. It was something special for just the two of us. Then one day, when he was about five, he said he was too old for nicknames like that. It hurt my heart to hear him say that, but I respected his wishes.

I am about to apologize for my accidental indiscretion when Forty-one wraps his arms around me. "See you later, big sis," he whispers.

An instant after Forty-one releases me, some of his classmates round the corner. I throw my brother a quick surreptitious smile and head back in the direction I came, toward the hospital.

MONDAY, JUNE 27
0845

JACKIE

I wish I could go back home. To tell everyone what happened to Ray. To discuss with the Elders what precautions we should take, what plan of action we should pursue. But I'm afraid that I don't want to hear the answers.

Last I spoke with them, the Elders were furious about the loss of their hostages. They had been planning to incorporate Ryan and Murphy into our society. Ryan already had a good reason to stay. He fathered at least thirty children during his time at our compound. Three of them were born prior to his escape, although Ryan had not yet been introduced to the infants.

Murphy was supposed to be married to Jose. The two had developed a relationship, and she seemed dedicated to him. After the wedding, it was planned for Jose to quickly impregnate her, ensuring her permanent attachment to us.

Now that the hostages are gone, unrest has plagued our

people. They want action. Or at the very least, new hostages. The Elders are already planning our next attack, but with the military's new security measures and travel restrictions, anything we attempt will be fraught with obstacles. And I don't want to be a part of it.

It is not that I am afraid of failure. I am not. But I refuse to put any more people at risk. Too many individuals lost their lives in our previous attacks, both my people and theirs. Some were those who I cared for, the others I have come to know afterward through their grieving friends and colleagues. It wasn't right to put any of these people in jeopardy, but it was especially wrong to risk harming the warriors. They serve the enemy, but not intentionally. They have no knowledge that our people die of illness and diseases that they could prevent.

Murphy saw the truth. According to Jose, she was changed by it. She wanted to help us. She could have been our strongest weapon yet.

But Murphy's determination to resolve the injustices that we suffer has been washed away. Because now she remembers nothing of her time with my people. Her innocence has been returned to her.

And our hope for the future has been lost.

MONDAY, JUNE 27
0850

SIX

Being in the hospital feels strange. But that doesn't make any sense at all. I practically grew up here—visiting my parents at work whenever we were allowed. About a year ago, when I came to the hospital on my first day as a student doctor, I immediately felt at home. I already knew the nurses and the layout of the wards. I understood how the medical records system worked and I'd watched other doctors do their morning rounds many times. I slid easily into the hospital routine as if I belonged here, which is odd because the Decision Makers chose Seven to be a doctor and me to be a warrior.

Ever since I came back from Up There, it feels like something about this white, sterile place is wrong. It seems *too* clean and *too* neat, but of course a hospital must be so and that's the way it has always been.

For some reason, the hospital bothers me now. I'm not

sure why. But it does.

Very deeply.

SEVEN

My visit with Doctor Johnson lasts so long that I completely miss the first lecture of the morning and barely make it to the seat Ten saved for me in our underwater classroom in time for the second lecture of the day to begin. The windows that look out into the ocean are dimmed, as they usually are during our lectures, probably to draw our attention away from the fish and swaying plant life beyond them.

"How was rehab?" Ten whispers to me, looking concerned.

Before I can answer, the professor announces, "Instead of our usual lecture, we are going to embark on an educational mission."

A mission? Ten told me that ever since our aerial drone was ambushed, all nonessential travel has been suspended. Perhaps the professor is referring to some sort of mission

47

within the compound. It is quite large and we haven't visited much of it yet.

The professor continues, "This morning, you will travel to a time before you were born. A time when your grandparents were children."

Time travel? The thought excites me while, at the same time, I feel uncertainty. I've read books where people travel through time. But those were fairy tales. I never imagined that time travel was something that people could actually do. Then again, it seems that a lot of what I read about in fairy tales really exists.

The woman continues, "You will now break into small groups. Please check the graphic above for your assignments. Your instructors will provide you with further information."

A few of our first year instructors enter the room. Among them is Ryan.

I look at the text now hanging above the empty podium, and I find my name. I am pleased to see that I am in Ryan's group, along with Ten, and … *Twelve. Twelve is in our group.*

I steel myself and head with Ten to Ryan. By the time we arrive at Ryan's side, Twelve is standing there waiting for us. I never told Ryan about my long history of bullying at the hands of Twelve, but I think he has sensed my discomfort around him.

"All right, group," Ryan says. "Come with me."

He leads us upstairs and takes us down the hallway that leads to the gymnasiums. The other groups travel this way as well. Ryan chooses a gymnasium door and scans it open, then he scans it closed behind us so that our group is the only one inside. The room is devoid of all equipment except for four thick black jumpsuits hanging on the wall and four helmets.

"It is extremely important that you follow my instructions at all times," Ryan says, as he passes out the jumpsuits.

"Why is it so important to follow your instructions, sir?" Twelve asks. "What could happen to us?"

"Just do as I say, Howard," Ryan says, deadly serious.

"Yes, sir," Twelve mumbles, averting his gaze.

Ryan instructs us to put on the black jumpsuits. It seems that his warning to follow instructions is the only additional information he is going to share, but I suppose I should have expected that. We are rarely told more than we need to know.

The jumpsuits remind me of the ones we wore when we left the warrior compound for the first time. Padded and thick. To protect us from injury. The suits envelop us from head to toe, even covering our shoes. Once we have finished pulling the protective jumpsuits over our warrior ones, Ryan hands us each a helmet, keeping one for himself. His forehead is creased and his body stiff with tension. I wonder why he seems uneasy, but I don't have the chance to ask any questions, because Ryan is already instructing us to put on our helmets. Then he tells us to hold onto one another's hands.

We form a circle. My padded hands holding onto Ryan's and Ten's. Ten's holding mine and Twelve's. Twelve's holding Ten's and Ryan's. For almost a minute, everything goes black, as if I've closed my eyes inside a room with no illumination. And then, energy surges through my every nerve. And the darkness disappears.

We are no longer in the gymnasium. We are standing on a black, hard, bumpy path flanked by crumbling structures that extend all the way up to the clouds and disappear into them. The sky is an eerie mix of yellow, brown, and gray—rather than blue—giving the appearance of a strange cross between night and day. The sun above us is red, the color of blood. The air is filled with the horrid pungent odor of excrement mixed with something I can't identify. Crunchy broken things crack under my feet with each footstep. Sounds of misery fill my ears.

There are people everywhere. They are all much too thin and their hair is mussed and matted. They look hungry, but not in a way I've ever seen before. It looks as if they haven't eaten for weeks. A man brushes against me. He turns and coughs right at me. Droplets of fluid spew from his mouth and nose. I recoil, falling against Ryan, who is standing beside me. Ten steps between me and the man.

"Careful," Ryan says to us.

The man who coughed doesn't acknowledge my presence or Ten's. He just keeps on walking, almost aimlessly, down the black path. I wipe the droplets from my face shield with the back of my arm.

"Are these people Outsiders?" I whisper to Ryan.

"They're just *people*," Ryan says. "There are no Outsiders yet ... well, not exactly."

Ryan, Ten, Twelve, and I stick close together, weaving our way around the strangers as we make our way along the path. It isn't easy. The path is badly damaged and so it must be tread carefully to avoid tripping and falling, and many of the people here are unsteady on their feet. Most seem ill, but with what I can't tell. I've never seen anyone so ill as this still walking around.

Ryan leads us closer to some of the structures alongside the path. At the ground level, these structures have large glass windows ... or, more correctly, *had* glass windows. The window glass is broken and litters the ground. Past the windows, I see lots of empty shelves. The ground beneath them is covered in broken things, lots of broken things. "What is this place?" I ask Ryan.

"We'll talk later," he says, sounding distracted. "For now, just observe and keep moving."

Twelve opens his mouth as if to speak, but then his eyes go wide, and he points behind me.

"RUN!" Ryan shouts.

Ten grabs my hand and we race with Ryan as a ball of fire erupts about fifty feet over my left shoulder. Some of the strangers are running along with us, but most aren't. They must be too weak. I hear pained guttural screams in our wake. When I look back, the fire is mostly gone. The majority of the people who remain are lying on the ground. Some appear to be alive, but barely. I start back toward them, but Ryan grabs my arm.

"We need to help them!" I say. Even though we have no medical supplies, we could at least staunch some of the blood flowing so freely from their pale bodies until help arrives.

"There's nothing we can do," Ryan says. "Keep moving. We need to go to that building over there." He points to a huge gray-white structure in the distance.

"What is it?" Twelve asks, speaking for the first time since we started our mission.

"It's a hospital," Ryan says.

I look back toward the wounded. Uninjured people have gathered to help them, but they aren't making any attempts to take the injured to the hospital about two hundred feet away. They seem only to be offering gestures of comfort. Helping the suffering people by consoling them during their transition from life to death.

I turn to Ryan. "Do they know there's a hospital here?" They must know. How could they not know where the hospital is?

"Yes," he says. "They know."

"Then why aren't they trying to save these people's lives?" I ask.

Ryan touches my arm, guiding me away from the dying, insistent that we continue what seems to be our urgent journey toward the hospital. "Keep moving," he says.

It makes my stomach feel sick to turn away from the wounded, but I trust Ryan. And so I reluctantly follow his orders. But I'm still not sure why we've come here. What we're supposed to do.

The professor told us that we would be traveling back to a time when our grandparents were children, and so I try to pay attention to the children. There are no babies here. The smallest child I see is a toddler, asleep in the arms of a man—her father, I guess. As I spot more and more children, I notice something. The expressions on their young faces don't match the situation around them. Any child in such a place as this should be frightened, sad, crying, but none of the small faces here hold any emotion at all. Their expressions are blank. Hopeless.

We approach the tremendous building that Ryan

identified as a hospital. What I'd thought were rows of windows on the upper levels are actually squares of gray metal secured to the building by silver bars. The base of the structure is obscured by tall, thick metal sheets. Soldiers dressed in dark green pants, shirts, and helmets, guard the hospital with their large weapons.

We are the only people who come near. All of the strangers have stopped about fifty feet away, as if held back by an invisible wall.

"Are you sure this is a good idea?" Twelve asks Ryan.

"It's what we need to do," Ryan says simply.

As we get close to the building, one of the soldiers raises his weapon, aiming it right at us. We leap out of the way. We have no weapons. Other than our helmets and thick jumpsuits, we are defenseless.

"HALT!" the soldier commands. But his weapon is no longer pointed at us. It remains fixed on something else … something behind us.

I turn and find one of the men who I saw earlier, the one with the sleeping toddler in his arms. Now that I see her up-close, I note that she is not sleeping. Her eyes are partly open and her breaths are too labored to be those of sleep. The man is about ten feet behind us. A few feet past where the other strangers have stopped.

"Please!" the man shouts to the soldiers in a hoarse, gravelly voice. "My baby needs help. Take her. I will stay out—" But he doesn't finish. An earsplitting burst of sound comes from the soldier's weapon and the man collapses backward, falling in a heap onto the ground, still cradling his child. A spot of blood has appeared right in the center of the man's forehead, but I don't know how it got there. I didn't see anything contact his head before it appeared. Could the weapon have caused it? I've never known a weapon to directly draw blood.

No one is coming to the man's assistance—they must be too afraid—and so I run to him.

"Murphy!" Ryan calls out to me, but I ignore him.

I kneel beside the fallen man and assess him. He is not breathing. He is hardly bleeding, but there is a wound on his forehead that appears to be so deep that whatever caused it must have penetrated his skull. His eyes are open, but they lack the spark of life. Even if I had the equipment to treat him, I don't think I could save this man.

I put my hand on his little girl's chest. My fingers slip into the deep groves between her ribs and I feel the rapid beating of her heart and her quick, desperate breaths.

"The girl's alive, but she needs help!" I shout back toward Ryan and Ten, but when I look up, I find them by my side, along with Twelve.

I try to lift the girl into my arms, but it is as if she's attached to her father and the ground, immovable. "I can't pick her up," I say, confused. *How could the girl be stuck to*

55

the ground?

"Come on, Murphy," Ryan says.

"Why can't I pick her up?" I ask Ryan, tears pooling in my eyes.

"You can't manipulate this environment," he says. "You can only experience it."

"So it's not real?" I ask.

"It *was* real," he says. "But it's not happening now. And so you can't change it."

I try again to lift the child to no avail. "But it *did* happen. To our grandparents."

"Yes," Ryan says.

"This girl could be my grandmother," I say.

"She isn't," Twelve says.

"How do you know?" I shout at him. "How do you know she's not *your* grandmother? She has black hair, just like you." I touch the girl's stringy hair, it feels silky beneath my fingertips, but it doesn't move like hair ordinarily would.

"Because that child isn't going to survive," he says coolly.

The child's lips are now rapidly turning bluish-purple. Her desperate breaths have ceased. My mind swims with all the medical interventions I could take to keep her alive. But I can't save her. We exist in different times. There is nothing I can do to intervene. I can only sit with her, helpless, and feel her heartbeats come slower and slower.

Until they don't come at all.

"She's dead," I say.

"We need to move," Ryan says, his eyes pained.

Ten helps me to my feet, and together the four of us walk toward the hospital. The soldiers guarding the entrance ignore us as we approach.

"They can't see us," Ryan tells us.

We make our way through a small opening in the metal sheets and enter a large, dimly-lit room filled with people ... mostly children ... in various stages of illness. Many are struggling to breathe.

Every bed, every chair, nearly every available spot on the floor is occupied by a sick child. There must be about two hundred children here. Only about a dozen adults are in the room. The men and women wear light-blue pants and undershirts, along with yellow smocks protecting their clothes. Clear goggles cover their eyes and white masks shield their mouths and noses.

There aren't enough adults to tend to all of the children. Instead, less-ill older children care for sicker younger ones, and some younger children provide comfort to ailing older children. It makes my throat squeeze tight to think of my little brother being forced to care for me because I was too ill to care for myself, because I was dying.

That's what these children are doing. They aren't recovering from their illnesses. They are dying. This is no hospital. This is a nightmare.

TEN

"How did they get so sick?" Seven whispers to Ryan.

"They have influenza," he says. "It's a type of viral infection. This particular strain caused fulminant pneumonia in eighty percent of those affected."

"How did they treat it?" Seven asks.

Ryan shakes his head. "In most cases, they didn't. There wasn't enough treatment to go around."

"Where are our grand—?" Twelve starts, but his question is interrupted by a deafening BOOM! It seems to have come from outside the hospital, but the walls, the floor, the ceiling, everything shakes. A few of the children scream, but most are too far gone to even flinch.

"What was that?" Twelve asks, his gaze darting around.

Ryan leads us toward the exit. "Come with me."

"No!" Twelve says. "Whatever's happening out there,

I don't want to have any piece of it." He starts away from us.

"HOWARD, COME NOW!" Ryan commands.

But Twelve keeps walking away. And then there is an odd whistling sound.

"GET DOWN!" Ryan shoves Seven and me to the floor.

Heat. It's everywhere. Burning my skin. Penetrating my flesh. A sickening smell pours down my throat, choking me. I hold my breath until the heat subsides, leaving my skin stinging painfully in its wake. Cautiously, I take a searing breath and assess my injuries. My ears throb. My head aches. Large hunks of rock pin me flat on my back.

"Murphy!" I call out. My voice echoes inside my head. It's as if my ears are underwater.

"Hanson!" Seven screams. I can barely hear her, but the pain in her voice is clear.

It takes some work to turn my head toward her due to the weighty chunks that cover my chest and the intense burning in my skin when I move. Once I am facing her, I see a metal cabinet, almost as big as she is, resting on her back, holding her down.

With my legs, I push at the cabinet until it shifts and one end bangs to the floor. Ryan heaves it the rest of the way off of her. He helps her to her feet, and I finally see her body. Her jumpsuit has been burned away in spots. Her exposed skin is red and raw. Bloody metallic bits have stuck into her flesh. Ryan's skin has similar injures to Seven's. I assume mine does too.

Seven and Ryan quickly get to work unburying me. They get something off my chest and I can breathe freely again.

"Your arm!" Seven says with barely a sound.

I sit up, wincing against the soreness in my ribs, and look down at my left arm. It is now completely severed from my body.

It's not real, I tell myself. *It's not real.* But the pain is. The pain is very real. I can even feel the blood oozing from the stump of my arm and dripping down my chest.

"Go take shelter in the door frame!" Ryan orders us. "I'll be right there!"

I grab Seven's hand with my remaining one and we run as fast as our battered bodies can, straight to the place where we entered the hospital just minutes ago. Lying on the ground are some of the soldiers we passed earlier, now bloodied and unconscious. Some are taking weak breaths. Some don't breathe at all.

Seven puts her arms around me. Her embrace hurts, but I try not to show it, because as much as it hurts, I want her close to me. "I can't feel your left arm," she says. "Is it actually gone?"

"No, it's still there," I say. But that's just a hope, not a certainty.

I look back the way we came and see Ryan walking toward us, carrying Twelve. Twelve is more bloodied than the rest of us and his breathing is quick and forced. He's mumbling at Ryan, "… then how do we stop this?"

Ryan shakes his head. "We can't."

MONDAY, JUNE 27
0949

SEVEN

Ryan keeps Twelve in his arms, like an infant, as he follows Ten and me through the exit. Nothing could have prepared me for what I see outside the hospital. The place where we were just moments ago is dead. Everyone. Everything. As far as my eyes can see. Men, women, and children. Thousands of lifeless bodies littering a vast wide-open space. If there are any who aren't dead, they give no indication.

"Who did this?" I ask.

"Those who wanted what we had," Ryan says.

As we walk past the deceased people and the broken structures that no longer reach the sky, I keep hold of Ten's hand. I ignore the agonizing pain in my skin that is worse where our hands contact each other, and I disregard my deep instinct to avoid public touch. I guess the latter shouldn't matter, Ryan has seen Ten and I touch, and

Twelve's eyes are shut and his face tight with pain. He is too injured to care.

"Why did we come here?" I ask, possibly not even aloud. But Ten answers.

"*This* is The War," he says. "The one we've been told about ever since we were children. It might be over now, but it *was* real."

Suddenly, everything fades into blackness. And then I hear Ryan's voice.

"Please remove your helmet," he says. "The Sim is complete."

MONDAY, JUNE 27
1000

TEN

As my eyes adjust to the bright light of the gymnasium, my gaze finds Seven's. She looks at my left arm. It is fully intact and uninjured. Seven strokes it with her fingers, perhaps to be sure that it is okay, before she turns her attention to removing her bulky jumpsuit—which is now whole again, undamaged, as is mine. Ryan is a few feet away, helping Twelve remove his suit. Twelve looks as if his mind has gone absent, the same way he appeared after our terrestrial drone was attacked.

Peeling the jumpsuit from my sore body sends fresh waves of pain through my nerves. Where the suit no longer contacts my skin, the pain lessens, although it does not entirely disappear. An unsettled feeling remains in my gut too—not from any injuries, but from the history that I just witnessed. The insight into the life of those who came before us.

Once Ryan has returned the jumpsuits and helmets to the hooks on the gymnasium wall, he sits on the floor beside us. "Does anyone have any questions?" he asks.

My brain is far too busy processing my experience to formulate any coherent questions. We have just come back from The War. Somehow it was exactly like I'd envisioned. But it's one thing to envision the horrific. It's another thing to witness it firsthand. I guess Seven and Twelve are still processing things as well, because neither of them gives any response to Ryan's question.

"All right then," Ryan says. "On your feet."

MONDAY, JUNE 27
1010

SEVEN

In a daze, I follow Ryan into the airlock. If what we
just experienced was real, then it is no wonder that our
great grandparents agreed to take their children down into a
box under the ground. Anything would be better than the
life they had here.

I imagine what it was like for our grandparents as
small children, scared numb, to be taken for the first time
into our box. How wonderful it must have seemed to them.
Clean and safe. With plenty of food to eat and comfortable
places to rest. With beautiful music to listen to and pretty
pictures to look at. Free of blood and death. An escape from
their nightmares.

The airlock door opens and Ryan leads us down the
ramp and onto the sand. The rest of our classmates are
already sitting on the beach, staring blankly at the ocean.

My eyes scan the unoccupied sand to our right. Then I

realize what I'm looking for. The blood of the soldier who was attacked this morning. The blood is gone now. Either cleaned away or covered with sand.

Ten and I head over to where Thirteen, Nineteen, and Twenty-two are sitting. Ryan goes to stand with the other instructors. Twelve walks in the opposite direction of everyone else and then sits on the sand alone.

After Ten and I settle down, Nineteen is the first to speak. "That was the most awful thing I've ever experienced," she says, without taking her eyes off the ocean. Crashing waves fill the silence that follows. The sound is violent, but strangely soothing.

"I guess they're trying to demonstrate the successes of the warrior program," Twenty-two finally responds. "Maybe they're trying to lead us to believe that, however horrible we might think it is up here right now, it was once much worse."

Out of the corner of my eye, I see Ryan separate himself from the other instructors and start heading away from all of us. My mind flashes to what Doctor Johnson told me this morning about what happened to Six while she was imprisoned with Ryan. I need to get some answers, and if I want to ask Ryan about Six's experience with the Outsiders, I need to do it where no one else will hear us.

"I'll be right back," I say to my friends, as I get to my feet.

"You okay?" Ten asks me.

"I'm fine." I leave before he can ask anything further.

Ryan spots me jogging toward him. He stops and waits for me to approach. When I finally arrive, I am breathless, but he doesn't wait for me to recover before he starts on his way. His speed is slow though, so it's easy to keep pace with him. "I suppose you came up with some questions," he says.

I swallow. "Yes."

"All right, let's hear them."

"What happened to me when we were imprisoned by the Outsiders?" I ask. Ryan knows perfectly well that it was Six—not me—who was captured by the Outsiders, but I ask the question this way in case someone is somehow listening.

Ryan picks up his pace a little. "What brought that on?" he asks. He clearly would have preferred questions about our war experience.

"Doctor Johnson told me that I was tortured mentally and physically," I say. "I need to know what they did to me." I need to know this so that I can figure out if Six will be able to get past it. I guess all I really need to know about is the first nine weeks of her captivity, since that's all she will remember. Maybe I should phrase my question differently—

"I suppose being imprisoned in a tiny room is a form

of torture," Ryan says. "But other than that, you weren't harmed. Not that I'm aware of. I wasn't with you all the time, but I don't think you could have completely hidden the aftereffects of abuse from me such that I never suspected it."

I step in front of him, causing him to stop short, and I look him in the eyes. "No one there hurt me?" I ask.

"Quite the contrary," Ryan says. "There was an Outsider boy, Jose, who you seemed to grow quite attached to. I think you might have fallen in love with him."

Six … in love with a *boy*? That doesn't sound right. But maybe under the stress of being held captive, she and Jose did develop a bond. If so, perhaps Six and Nine have a chance of growing together. Of becoming friends—

"Do you have any other questions?" Ryan asks me.

I shake my head. "I guess not."

"Good," he says, looking away. "I'd like a little time alone now. All right?"

"Of course," I say.

Ryan breaks into a jog and I start back toward my friends. I am certain that Ryan told me the truth as he knows it. Other than some of my fellow warriors, Ryan and Jackie are the only people who I fully trust up here who are still alive.

While I am relieved that Six was unharmed during her time with the Outsiders, now I am faced with a different concern: Doctor Johnson lied to me. Why would she tell me that I experienced unspeakable torture when I did not? Why would she falsely traumatize me, when she is supposed to be helping me to heal? Why would Doctor Johnson lie?

MONDAY, JUNE 27

1045

JACKIE

My navigator alerts me that we have a last-minute unplanned mission, which puts me on edge considering the events of early this morning. My pulse is beating rapid-fire as I enter the mission briefing room and take a seat with the other soldiers.

Lieutenant Commander Wong—a lanky older woman who wears her short, dark hair gathered in an orderly ponytail at the base of her neck—enters the room and sits at the head of the briefing table. The room instantly silences and Wong has our rapt attention.

"Good morning," she says. "I have some excellent news to report." Although there is no obvious response to her words, the anxious tension that fills the room is palpable. She continues, "While most of you were sleeping last night, the compound where Lieutenant Commander Ryan and warrior Murphy were held captive was destroyed, along with all those who lived there."

My body freezes with shock, and unbearable pain spins wildly inside my head. I want to scream my throat raw. I want to smash, kick, obliterate everything around me. *Everyone I grew up with. My family. My friends. Everyone who I love. They are all dead.*

It is only my frail wisp of a will to live that holds me still and silent, that forces me to control my breathing and my heartbeat, so that those who sit inches away from me can't sense my agony.

The other soldiers applaud. Some cheer. I force myself to applaud too.

For the murder of my loved ones.

Wong activates a graphic in the center of the table. A three-dimensional image of the fifty-three buildings that make up the community where I once lived rotates slowly around so we can see it from all sides. The buildings appear the way they did when last I saw them. Unharmed and intact.

I spot the house where I was raised. Like all of the homes in my community, the exterior appears forgotten, abandoned, with boarded-up windows and broken siding. Behind those walls is the room where I grew up. When I was six, my father reinforced the walls by lining them with blue tarp—because blue was my favorite color—and he painted pictures of rabbits and deer and trees and flowers in the spots where the windows should be, so I could pretend that I could look out on the forest. My father died six months later from pneumonia.

I loved that little blue room. It made me feel close to my dad. Now, the room belongs to my baby brother. Someday I will tell him that our dad … And then I remember. My baby brother is dead. He is dead now, along with my mother. And my two little sisters.

For an instant, I hold out hope that I somehow misheard Wong, or that she is mistaken. But then the image before me clicks to a different one. If I hadn't been staring so hard at my house, it would be impossible to figure out where it once was. Every home has been leveled and along with it, every tree within a five mile radius. All that is left of my community is rubble.

It is fortunate that everyone in the room is so focused on the graphic, because if they weren't, they'd surely see the pain in my face. How do you hide the hurt of watching your home—with everyone you love sleeping inside it—be annihilated in a single instant?

"The bodies have been collected by our cadaver drones and the area has been secured," Wong continues. "We're going to dispatch each of you, along with a team of support staff, to gather intelligence. We need to learn as much about our enemy as possible. This was just one of many tribes of Outsiders, but we think they were one of the most advanced and, therefore, one of the most dangerous. In addition to the recent attacks, we believe they were planning additional assaults on our military, and on civilians as well. We need to gather any and all potential sources of information before the site is terminally cleared. If in doubt, collect it." And then she posts a list of our names along with the drone we've been assigned to. "Please report to the hangar for immediate departure."

I feel myself stand and walk to the drone hangar. I find my assigned drone and sit in the pilot's seat. Right now, I am supposed to be reviewing the flight plan to prepare for departure, but my eyes blur as I gaze at the information on the screen and I can't read the words. It is a good thing that these drones fly themselves, because right now, I feel incapable of piloting anything, even myself.

As the robot soldiers on my team finish filing into the cabin, I click the "Accept" button on the flight information screen. The drone door shuts and locks, and the platform beneath us rises to position us for takeoff.

Blindly, I clear us for departure and our drone ascends into the cloudless sky. Tears pool in my eyes. If I need to cry, now is my chance. The robots in the seats behind me won't care. They are busy downloading their mission instructions. If I keep my breathing steady and my body relaxed, I won't draw any attention to myself. And so I take slow breaths and let the tears roll down my cheeks as, one at a time, I think of each of those who are gone—beginning with Ray, who is certainly dead by now. I allow myself a few moments to feel the loss of each of my loved ones, and to silently say goodbye.

When we are five minutes from landing, I surreptitiously wipe away my tears and focus my eyes out the front window, preparing myself for the hell I am about to face. And then I see it. A live version of the horrific graphic Wong showed us. I steel myself and concentrate on what I need to do. I can't risk revealing my pain. I need to protect my true identity, so that I can live to honor the memory of my loved ones.

Our drone touches down gently near the perimeter of the destruction. My support team of twelve robots follows me as I report to Wong for my instructions. "Area 36," she barks at me, tapping her navigator to mine. The coordinates of Area 36—an irregular rectangle that covers about five-percent of the search area—come up on my navigator instantly.

I relay the coordinates to my support team and our navigators guide us to our assigned spot. The robots begin an organized search of the grounds and I start my own search, doing as I have been tasked, looking for items that could contain intelligence that the robots might miss, anything that might hold information about how my people operated. About what we knew and how we knew it.

As my eyes scan the ground, what I see breaks my heart. A lovingly crocheted dress—about the right size for a toddler—singed black and caked with dirt. A pair of men's eyeglasses, their frames broken and the glass shattered. A pink baby blanket stained with blood. The robots won't care about these objects, and neither will the humans who orchestrated this attack. They don't care about the lives of the people they killed. *The Outsiders are the enemy.* The military wants us to collect documents, electronics, or devices that contain information about how my people planned our past attacks and what missions we were planning for the future, so they can protect themselves from other tribes of Outsiders. The ones who are still alive to pose a threat.

What the military seems not to realize is that any threat we posed to them was born from desperation. When we attacked, our plan was never to harm their people. Yes, a few of their people were killed and injured during our attacks. But that was not our intention. Up until this moment, I never had any desire to hurt their people, I just wanted so very desperately to help my own.

Sticking up out of the rubble, I spot a notebook. I lift the book and leaf through it. Coal drawings. Of the forest. Of a girl. A man. A bird perched in a tree. The drawings are stunning. So rich in detail and beauty that they move me almost to tears, but I can't let that happen. There are too many human eyes here that could see me.

I shut the book, place it gently on the ground, and flag it for the robots to pick up. This book doesn't contain any intelligence information. It holds only art. But whatever the robots collect here will be examined back at the base by humans. I want a human being to see those drawings. To know that they killed the beautiful mind that created them.

As I continue along, my foot catches on something: a hatch. The lock is still secured but the latch is severed. I lift the hatch, descend on the damaged ladder, and pull the hatch closed behind me, shutting out the light. While I appreciate the cloak of darkness, it will be impossible to navigate in the pitch black. I activate the illuminator at my waist and dial down the brightness to provide just enough soft blue light to see where I'm heading, no more.

The tunnels walls have crumbled from the force of whatever destroyed the buildings above, but mostly they are the way I remember from my childhood. As a child, I spent countless hours in these cool and damp tunnels with my best friend, Ray—the same person who I saw knocked bloody and unconscious on the beach early this morning. Ray showed me how to navigate these tunnels by using the little markings at each branch that provide information about what lies ahead. He didn't use the markings himself much though. He had the entire tunnel system memorized.

Ray and I used the tunnels as our second home. These

tunnels were where he taught me all kinds of skills. He taught me how to carve a stick into a flute. He taught me how to take broken things apart, fix them, and put them back together again. He even dragged a bicycle down here because I'd read a book where a girl rode a bicycle and I really wanted to try it for myself. Everyone said it was too dangerous to play on a bicycle outside. But Ray suggested that we take the rusted old bicycle that lived in my family's garage to the tunnels. The day that he taught me to ride that bicycle was the day we shared our first kiss.

Ray kindled my interest in infiltrating into the military as a way to help our people. Because he was one year my senior, he left first, but I followed in his footsteps. We were able to maintain our friendship once I arrived at the base, but of course, we had to keep our shared history a secret. We never spoke of our childhood adventures, but whenever I looked into his gray-blue eyes I could see that he hadn't forgotten them. My heart aches to know that I will never look into his eyes again.

My navigator beeps, indicating that I have crossed out of the borders of my assigned area. I am about to turn back when I notice a passageway that looks familiar. Different from the others, because it has doors that lead to living quarters. It's the passageway under the prison house. Jose's quarters are there.

I silence my navigator and proceed toward the doors.

All of them are open, which feels strange because their owners would never leave them that way. It was required that these doors remain closed at all times. The cadaver drones must have come through the tunnels as well as the areas above ground. That's good. I don't want to see my cousin's dead body.

Jose's quarters are not at all how I remember them. Unlike the tunnels, the effects of the military's attack are clearly evident here. The ceiling has fallen loose in places. Dirt and support beams are strewn about. Shelves are broken, their contents tossed onto the ground. The bed sheets are stained with blood.

The walls speak of Jose's life. Crayon drawings made by his little brother and sisters. Old magazine pages he salvaged that show towering silver skyscrapers. Dried leaves he collected from beneath an ancient oak tree with gorgeously gnarled branches. On the bedside table is his chess set with pieces carved by his father. These items were Jose's prized possessions. Once we are done gathering intelligence, they will all be destroyed, like he was.

I hear something crack on the ground behind me. I grab my weapon and whip around to find myself staring at a robot soldier. She is not from my support team, but she is one of "us." I lower my weapon immediately.

"This isn't your assigned area, Lieutenant," she says.

"I heard a sound come from this room," I lie to her. "I

came to investigate."

"And what did you find?" she asks.

I shake my head. "Nothing of importance."

My words are the truth. Everything important has been stripped from this world. All of the people who I love are gone from it. What remains here are objects that are of no worth, not to the military, not to anyone anymore. Without their owners, these items hold no value. Not even to me. All they do is stir up painful memories of those who have gone. Never to return.

MONDAY, JUNE 27
1756

SEVEN

Our final lecture of the day is just about finished when the commander appears in the doorway of the underwater classroom. The professor looks over at him, appearing surprised to see him here. She stops in mid-sentence and asks, "May I help you, Commander?"

"Please finish your lecture," he says in a quiet voice.

And so she does, but I have a feeling that she abbreviates her closing remarks. Although everyone is sitting upright in their chairs, facing straight ahead, appearing focused on the professor, everyone's minds are surely now on the commander.

Once the professor steps from the podium, the commander takes her place. "Ladies and gentlemen," he begins. "I have some important news to share. I trust you will find it comforting." I relax, but only a little. "As you know, nine months ago, we experienced some serious

Outsider attacks, one of which resulted in one of your colleagues being taken prisoner." I feel my cheeks burn with uneasiness as the commander continues, "Early this morning, this threat was neutralized. The Outsiders who attacked us have been eliminated."

"How did we neutralize the threat, sir?" Twelve asks. "How were they eliminated?"

I see a flash of what might be discomfort on the commander's face, and then he explains, "The Outsiders who attacked us lived in a compound, like this one, only much less advanced. This morning, we destroyed that compound."

"What about the people there, sir?" Thirteen asks.

"They were destroyed," the commander says, matter-of-factly.

"You killed them all, sir?" I ask, incredulous.

"Yes," he says.

"You shouldn't have done that, sir." After I speak, I realize how dangerous my statement is. Publicly challenging the commander's actions is certainly still against the rules, even now that we are full-fledged warriors.

The commander doesn't seem at all rattled. "The Outsiders presented an ongoing threat to public safety. After extremely careful analysis and consideration of our options, this was deemed the best course of action," he says. "Other factions may rise up and threaten us in the future, but our actions today will serve as a warning to them all. Those who attack us will be destroyed." And then his gaze softens and his eyes scan the faces of each and every one of us. "And you, my children, will be safe."

My gaze falls to my lap. The commander thinks of us as his children. He killed the Outsiders to protect us. To keep us safe. Wouldn't I do the same if someone was threatening my child? Wouldn't I attack anyone and everyone necessary in order to defend her? If the Outsiders had come so close to destroying her in the past, wouldn't I destroy them before they had another chance to cause her harm?

As horrible as it makes me feel inside, I think I would.

And so, although it still sounds wrong, maybe the military really did do what was right.

MONDAY, JUNE 27
1917

SIX

After dinner, I ask Three to take a walk with me. I want to be with her. Alone.

When I lead Three in the opposite direction of the plaza garden, she looks at me quizzically. "I thought we were going for a walk."

I lean close to her. "Are you willing to go somewhere forbidden?"

She looks into my eyes, searching them for information, and then she says, "I'll go anywhere with you."

And so I guide her to the entrance to the forbidden hallways, and I take out Forty-one's tag. Her eyes widen with fear as the door slides to the side, but she follows me into the shadowy hallways lit only by skinny blue lights along the edges of the floor. I scan the door closed behind us.

"Have you been in here before?" Three asks, the awe in her voice clear.

"Twice," I say.

"It's so dark and … beautiful," she whispers.

I smile. I want to embrace Three. But not here. I want to be somewhere more concealed. I take her to the wall that leads to the drone closet. After a few failed attempts to locate the hidden scanner, the wall finally slides to the right. Three inhales and enters the empty closet. After I scan the door closed, she turns to me.

"Is it private here?" she asks.

"Yes," I say.

She looks into my eyes. "May I touch you?" The only time we've ever touched before was a tiny, tingly tap of our hands that we did very quickly, to make it appear accidental to anyone who might see. We have never touched freely.

"Please touch me," I breathe.

Three places her hands on the sides of my face. I feel the heat of her energy. My own energy rises inside me, threatening to take over my brain. I shut my eyes, trying to stay in command of my breathing. Trying to keep my feelings in check. But they are already out of my power. All of the love that I feel for Three has come to the surface in a trembling teary mess.

Three wraps her arms around me so tenderly that my heart melts. Each breath brings our bodies closer together, but never close enough. Her hand moves to the zipper of my jumpsuit.

"May I—?" she starts.

I feel my body tense—anxious but alive with anticipation.

I let our gaze meet. "Yes."

MONDAY, JUNE 27
1910

SEVEN

After dinner, there is a movie in the recreation room, but Ten and I choose to forgo it. The majority of our classmates do as well, heading off to their quarters, mostly in pairs. Nineteen goes to Twenty-two's quarters. I'd sensed that they'd grown close during my time away, and so I am not surprised. Thirteen wishes Ten and me goodnight as she heads alone into her quarters, and Ten and I go into mine.

After I scan my door closed, Ten and I strip off our clothes and take comfort in each other's arms. We lose control in a way that I can only describe as desperate. It isn't scary and it doesn't hurt, but is the most violent that our losing control has ever been.

When we are through, Ten asks if I am okay.

"I guess," I answer. "Are you?"

"I guess," he says.

And then he lightly strokes my back until I drift off into a drained, exhausted sleep.

MONDAY, JUNE 27
1928

JACKIE

During my first years at the base, my quarters were located above the ocean, with those of the other enlisted soldiers, but now I live in officers' quarters. The tunnel that leads to my quarters is surrounded on all sides by ocean. Swaying kelp. Swimming fish. Sometimes otters, dolphins, seals, or sea lions dart in and out of view. The first time I walked through this tunnel, I was overcome by the beauty of it. I never thought I'd live anyplace this spectacular. Sometimes, it even felt a little bit like home. But never again.

I scan open the door to my quarters. The outer walls of the room reveal the dimming blue-green underwater world outside that will soon disappear along with the setting sun. I lie down on my bed, staring at the undulating strips of kelp, and I let my tears come unrestrained. No one can see me here. Not even the creatures of the ocean. The transparent walls that surround me are strictly one way.

My tears turn into sobs. I don't think I've ever cried like this. Of course I've lost friends and family over the years, and I cried for them. But those losses came one at a time. This time, I've lost so many all at once. I can't even begin to properly grieve.

I always thought that, one day, once I'd made a difference for my people, I'd go back home to them. But now I have no home to return to. The only life I have left is a false one, here among those who I don't trust. Those who I will never trust. Those who would destroy me if they ever found out who I really am.

If I wish to survive, I must ensure that my true identity is never discovered. I must erase all signs that I was once— and I will always be—an Outsider. I wipe my tears aside, slide my tablet from the desk, and activate it. On the home screen are icons for the various military-installed applications. I hover my finger over the "Rules and Regulations" icon and the document opens. On the tenth page, I place my third finger over a spot half of the way down and a quarter of the way across. The screen blinks, just for an instant, and I know to hold my finger still and gaze into the camera. My fingertip and retina are being scanned, confirming that I am an Outsider.

After a moment, an error message appears. I hover my finger over the lower left corner and the screen blinks off.

When it comes to life once again, I've reached my destination: a secret communication center. It is how I exchanged messages with the people back home. It's probably safest to remove it, so that its presence is never uncovered. Besides, it is useless now. There is no one left to communicate with.

I am about to start the deletion process when the screen flashes a string of garbled text. I recognize it as words written in code:

One unread message.

My heart squeezes tight with pain. The message must have been sent before—or during—the slaughter of my people. The author is now dead. The contents of this message may haunt me for the rest of my life, but I will not let these last words go unheard.

I open the message and more garbled text appears on the screen. Like all of our communications, it is encoded to protect its contents. I begin the work of deciphering the code. I don't dare to write it down. I can't risk recording it anywhere.

Finally, I make out the first line:

Compound attacked.

And then the next one:

Five survivors.

Below that are five additional lines of text. *The names of those who survived?* My entire being fills with hope. My heart pounds so hard that I think it might leap out of my chest.

Selena Brown. *A friend of my parents.*
Tamara Brown. *Selena's daughter.*
Kris Chang. *I grew up with him.*
Andrew Fishman. *He lives ... lived ... next door to my family.*
Jose Alvarez. *Jose. Jose!*

And so my mother and my siblings are dead, just as I thought. A realization that breaks my heart all over again. But Jose ... Jose is alive. Or at least he was alive when this message was written. The time code is from just after three this morning.

Carefully, I enter an encoded message in response. Hoping that it will be received:

Ray was taken prisoner by military.
I'm still here.

What can I do to help?

.

MONDAY, JUNE 27
2015

SIX

Three and I don't speak as we put back on our underwear and jumpsuits. She finishes first and goes to sit against the wall. Once I am dressed, I join her, sitting close enough that our bodies touch. I feel incredibly relaxed. More than I have ever been I think. It is as if my insides fell completely apart and then came back together again in a new, calm, peaceful state.

"What was it like above the sky?" Three whispers.

Suddenly I feel naked again, but this time instead of feeling excited, I feel intensely vulnerable. Up There is the one thing I can't share with Three. First, because hearing that I spent most of my time locked in a small room guarded by frightening men with weapons would cause her pain. But also because I can't tell her about the boy who visited me while I was in that room. A boy I might have fallen in love with. I can't tell Three about Jose.

"I don't remember very much of it," I say.

Her forehead creases. "What do you mean?"

I stare at the floor. "Just after I left, there was an accident. I was traveling inside a huge aerial drone and the drone crashed. They took me to the hospital and when I woke up, it was time to come back home." That isn't exactly a lie. All of those things happened, but I left out the parts in between. The parts that Three must never know.

"Were you injured?" she asks, her brow furrowed with concern.

I take a quick breath to steady my voice. "Not permanently."

Three touches my hand, sending a tingling up my fingers and into my chest. "I was so worried about you while you were gone. I woke up sweaty and cold from the nightmares about all the horrible things that might happen to you." Her gaze falls away from me. "I know I shouldn't tell you that … what if someday you have to go back and—"

"I won't have to go back," I reassure her, while attempting to reassure myself. "Everything's the way it should be now. I won't leave you ever again." I pull Three into my arms, holding her tight, feeling the comfort of her body against mine, but my mind slips back to last night's dream. I am in The White Room, mating with Jose, my feelings for him just as strong as the ones I feel now for

Three.

I shove the memory of my dream back, but I can't push away the questions it brings. Did I love Jose in real life? Did I mate with him after my memories fade away into nothingness? Did I want to?

It would probably be best if I forgot all about Jose. I will never see him again. I will never know how I felt about him. I will never know whether he became my friend, or my love, or even my torturer. But I can't seem to release him from my mind. For some reason, he is bonded there so strongly that I don't think even a full memory wipe could erase him.

Maybe I did love Jose. Otherwise why can't I let him go?

TUESDAY, JUNE 28
0015

JACKIE

I've been lying in bed for hours, but I feel as if sleep will never come. Outside my window, bioluminescent squid periodically speed through the underwater world, like shooting stars in the dark night sky. For the fiftieth time tonight, I check my hidden communication center, but there is no message in response to mine.

Perhaps those five remaining lives are now lost.

No. I can't think that way. There are other alternatives. The device that the survivors were using might have lost its ability to communicate. Or, more likely, the survivors are preoccupied. Focusing their attention on their continued existence.

I must do the same. My survival is far from assured. I am not safe here. I am living among enemies. Not everyone here is my enemy. Some don't deserve blame: the warriors, most of the soldiers, all of the support staff. These people are kept ignorant and are therefore largely innocent of culpability. But there are those here who made a conscious, unconscionable decision to murder innocent men, women, and children just because they were Outsiders.

Yes, there were bad Outsiders as well as good ones, but the military didn't discriminate. They killed all the good people back home. The people who I was trying to protect. I can never right that wrong, but I will find justice.

I'm just not sure how I'll be able to do it alone.

All of the Elders are dead. The five surviving Outsiders—if they are in fact still alive—won't be able to offer much assistance. I am on my own here.

Or maybe I'm not.

Suddenly, I realize where to turn.

Nine months ago, when we were planning Murphy's mission to get her back home, I learned that her boyfriend, Hanson, is quite the hacker. I'm not sure of the full extent of his abilities, but perhaps if we combine forces he could access the information that I need. At least he's worth a try. Even if we fail, I don't think he'd tell anyone what I asked of him.

I have kept his secrets. He should be willing to keep mine.

TUESDAY, JUNE 28
0517

SEVEN

I awaken with a knot in my gut, knowing that, in less than two hours, I'll have to face another session of rehab. I'm fairly certain that I can avoid Carter's wrath by obeying her commands. As long as I do as she says, I should have nothing to fear. Still, a sick feeling grips my stomach, rising up into my throat and—

"What's wrong?" Ten asks me.

I open my eyes and find him awake beside me, working on his tablet.

"I'm not looking forward to rehab," I say.

He turns toward me. "What happened there yesterday?"

I skip over my experience with Carter and go right to what is bothering me the most. "They had me talk to a doctor … I think she was a psychiatrist. She told me that while I was held prisoner by the Outsiders, they tortured me mentally and physically." Ten's eyes narrow. "But that isn't true," I add. "Ryan said Six wasn't abused at all. It makes me wonder if the memory wipe wasn't to protect her. Maybe it was to protect the people in charge."

"Protect them from what?" he asks.

"I don't know," I say. "But if they wipe people's memories in order to shield them from psychological trauma, why wouldn't they have wiped our memories after the terrestrial drone attack?"

"Ryan said that they use the memory wipe for *prolonged* trauma," Ten says. "The brain can probably compensate better for brief suffering than for sustained abuse."

"Then why do they wipe women's memories of their childbirths?" I ask.

Ten touches my cheek. "You don't remember Fifty-two's birth?"

"No." I feel an ache in my chest, a longing to remember. "My mom said they wiped her memories of our births as well. I guess they do it to all women. But no matter how bad the trauma of childbirth, I can't imagine that it is worse than the pain I felt at seeing Ma'am die at the hands of another. And if they're so intent on protecting us from trauma, why would they take us into that war Sim, telling us that it really happened, that our grandparents lived in that horrific time?"

Ten's grip on me tightens. "They're traumatizing us exactly the way they want to. They're controlling our experiences. Picking and choosing them. Deleting them if they don't serve their purposes or if they are at cross-purposes."

"So what are they trying to hide?" I ask.

Ten inhales. "We need to find out."

TUESDAY, JUNE 28
0548

TEN

While Seven was away, I spent a lot of time searching for useful information in the encrypted files hidden on my tablet. I have only been able to access a small fraction of them, but among the documents I found was an interactive schematic representation of the warrior compound. It maps out all of the areas we've been allowed into, but also the numerous places to which we've never been granted access. I turn the screen of my tablet to reveal it to Seven.

She stares at the information on the screen, entranced. "You found a map of the warrior compound!"

I scroll down to reveal a second map. "There are two levels, one above the water, but there's also an entire level below the water's surface."

She hovers her finger over one of the underwater conference rooms and a zero appears.

"That's how many people are in the room," I explain. I zoom in on the hallway containing our dormitories and hold my finger over Seven's quarters. The number "2" appears.

"It knows there are two people in here," Seven says with a shiver.

"No one needs a map to know that," I say.

She gives me a reluctant smile. "I guess you're right."

She zooms the graphic out and tries some of the gymnasiums. No people. No people. No people. No people. And the conference rooms. No one. No one. No one.

I point to the room labeled "Administration Control Center." "That's the commander's office," I say. As my finger hovers over it, the number "12" appears.

"*Twelve* people in the commander's office before morning reveille?" she asks. "What are all those people doing in his office at this hour?"

"That's what I want to know." At any hour, twelve people packed into the commander's office seems strange. If he were holding a meeting with more than five or six people, I would think he'd schedule it in a more accommodating room. "Every morning for the past week, he's held some sort of meeting there, with anywhere from nine to twelve people in attendance."

"Can you see their names?" Seven asks.

"No. Or at least I haven't figured out how to do that yet."

"So when are we going to go exploring with your chip?" Seven asks me.

"You want to go exploring?" The last time we discussed using my chip to gain access to restricted areas of the compound, Seven forbade it. She said it was too risky.

"How else are we going to find out what they're hiding?" she asks me now.

This time, I am the one who hesitates. While the prospect of a new adventure excites me, I'm concerned about the dangers it might bring. "If we get caught, who knows what they'll do to us," I say.

Seven looks into my eyes. "I have a feeling that, even if we obediently follow every rule, we can't avoid danger here. Something important is being hidden from us and we need to know what it is. Maybe it's better to take a risk. To do something 'bad' rather than to wait for something worse to be done to us."

"We'll start planning tonight," I say. And with that I agree to our new mission.

Seven wraps her arms around me and I hold her tight, knowing that any risk we take could cause us to lose each other in the process. But, if our suspicions are correct, even if we do nothing our safety is far from assured. Our new mission will offer more danger than I was hoping to have to face for the entire rest of our lives. But we need to uncover the truth.

Knowing the truth may be the only way to ensure our survival.

TUESDAY, JUNE 28
0600

SIX

My navigator wakes me for Fifty-two's morning feeding an hour before my normal wake up time, the same way it does every morning. Although I would probably benefit from an extra hour of sleep, I'm glad to have this time to organize my thoughts before I have to start the day.

Careful not to disturb Nine, I slide out of our bedroom capsule with Fifty-two and her bottle. I sit on the gathering room couch and cuddle her in my arms as she drinks down her formula in quick bursts of sucks and swallows. When she is through, I hold her on my shoulder and burp her, the way Nine taught me. Babies' stomachs are so little that even a small amount of air inside can cause the infant to spit out some of her precious milk, and it's important that she retains every drop. We are only presented with her allowed amount at each feeding, no more.

After she lets out a small burp, I settle her in my lap.

Often, she falls asleep after her feedings, but this morning she is wide awake. Her gaze locks into mine and she gives me a huge smile. My eyes blur instantly with tears.

"You're beautiful, you know that," I tell her. "We're not supposed to use that word to describe people, but I will anyway for you."

Fifty-two makes a soft cooing sound, as if she has understood my words.

"Can I tell you something else?" I have her undivided attention, and so I continue, "Every time I look at you, I see your mommy. I wish you could have spent more time with her, but maybe it's better that you won't remember her. That way you won't know what you lost. You won't miss her every moment. Like I do." I inhale, trying to hold back the tears that have already started to flow. "I miss your mommy so much."

I hear a rustling sound come from the bedroom capsule door. Nine is sitting there in the doorway, tears filling his eyes. He slides out of the capsule and sits uneasily next to us.

"I miss her too," he whispers. After a moment he adds, "I'm sorry I was listening. I shouldn't have—"

I cover his hand with mine. "It's okay."

Nine looks at me, his forehead wrinkled. "That's the first time you've touched me without being required to do so."

Guilt fills my throat. I was never purposely unkind to Nine, but I have not been a proper pair to him. He deserves better than what I've given him. "I'm sorry about the way I treated you in the past," I say. "I'm going to try to do better now."

"Up There changed you, didn't it?" he says.

I nod. "It did."

"Are you ever going to tell me about it?" he asks.

I consider his question, but only for a moment before I answer, "Yes."

Nine is the only one to whom I can tell everything that happened to me above the sky. He is the only person who, rather than being distracted by hurt or pain, will be able to help me make sense of what I experienced. And I know Nine will never share my secrets. He's already kept safe the very powerful ones that have been entrusted to him.

And so I begin, "I left our compound on a huge aerial drone, big enough to hold dozens of people. It flew us up into a night sky like the one above the plaza, except that this sky went on forever and ever. But then the drone fell from the sky. It crashed in a tremendous garden with towering trees, where the Outsiders found us. They locked me in a tiny room with a thick door that was guarded at all times by men with big weapons. I was scared. I thought I was going to die. Until I met Jose ..."

TUESDAY, JUNE 28
0655

SEVEN

I arrive early for rehab to avoid Carter's first opportunity to punish me. Her voice greets me through the communication system. She sounds pleased to see me, but I fail to find any reassurance in that. Even pleasant voices can be used to deliver nastiness. Twelve taught me that at an early age. He often administered his abuse in a saccharine tone.

"Are we ready?" Carter asks me.

"Yes," I say.

She turns away and walks me back to that awful purple pod. After I am undressed down to my underwear, Carter smiles and says, "We'll start off with some passive stretching. Go ahead and lie down."

I do as instructed, and Carter attaches the mask and wires. Once she is done, the pod takes hold of me and begins to manipulate my joints. I try to relax and let it do its job, because that seems to be what the pod prefers. Somehow it seems to sense when my joints are at their limits. It brings them just to that point, then holds them for a moment before it lets them return to neutral.

Once I am deemed adequately stretched, Carter puts some clear goggles over my eyes and says that we are going to do some strength training. *What are the goggles for?* I wonder, but too soon I get my answer.

The lining of the pod swells all around me, surrounding my body completely. It is as if I am being swallowed by water in some sort of strange purple swimming pool, pulled under a surface that I was floating on moments ago. The pod lining is nearly transparent and so, even though my head is now surrounded by it, I can still see a slightly-distorted version of my surroundings. But if it were not for the air flowing through the mask affixed to my face, I would surely die from lack of oxygen. And that makes me extremely anxious. I don't like Carter holding me in this type of position, one from which she controls my ability to live. No longer am I just trying to avoid punishment, I am trying to stay alive.

Despite the icy fear growing inside me, I tell my mind to stay calm. I force my breathing to be slow and easy, and I keep my heart rate steady. I feel like it is in my best interest not to let Carter see my discomfort, and with all the monitors attached to me, hiding my feelings won't be easy.

"I want you to work your muscles against the resistance of the pod," Carter says. Even though the pod lining covers my ears, I hear her clearly. "Whatever it does to you, I want you to do the opposite. Let's start with your feet."

The pod pushes my feet down. If I were standing on a floor, I'd be in tiptoe position.

"Bring your feet back up toward your body," Carter instructs.

I contract the muscles that counteract the downward movement, bringing my feet back to a neutral position.

"Very good," Carter says.

We do this exercise nine times more, before we move on to a different set of muscles. Slowly, we work our way up my body. As with the stretches, the pod seems to know my limits. It pushes me just to them, no more, no less. Each group of muscles is given ten repetitions of the same movement with a brief relaxation period in between. It is not unlike the strength training we've done during PT, except that here I am at the mercy of a pod … and, therefore, Carter. No matter who was at the controls, I would feel uneasy inside this big purple bubble, but I don't know Carter well enough to feel certain about my well-being.

"Keep calm," she says.

An order. One that I must obey. How will she punish

me if I don't comply?

As if the pod wishes to demonstrate its answer to this question, it swells a bit further, compressing me deeper inside it. My chest can no longer fully expand. And, therefore, neither can my lungs. If my lungs can't adequately inflate, it doesn't matter how much oxygen is pumping into the mask on my face. I will die.

I take a slow breath—as deep as my compressed chest will allow—and the pod loosens its grip. I fight the urge to take another desperate breath of air to make up for the prior inadequate one. Instead, I count off a full five seconds before I allow myself to take a gentle, easy breath.

Carter doesn't acknowledge what the pod did to me, a demonstration that was most certainly under her control. Neither do I.

Once my entire body has been tested, the pod lining mercifully decompresses. Then the pod lifts me to my feet. *What's next?* I wonder anxiously.

Carter attaches the shocker band to my waist, and I almost feel joyful. After the worry that I would be compressed to death by the pod, receiving a shock seems like a minor inconvenience, not worthy of a second thought.

"Let's do some jogging," Carter says. "Just keep pace with the treadmill."

Her barely-veiled threat isn't lost on me. *Don't worry,* I want to say. *I understand how this works. I do as you say, and I don't get hurt.*

The treadmill starts moving. I move with it, but my mind remains focused on my last thought. I look around the room at the other patients— people who are recovering from severe injuries or major surgeries, everyone here is obviously in need of intensive physical therapy. I don't belong here. Even if I had actually undergone Six's entire memory wipe procedure, even if I had been unconscious and lying in a hospital bed for weeks, physical therapy shouldn't be necessary at all. The Stim suit is more than adequate for maintaining muscle conditioning. A modified workout program should be all that is required to return me to my previous state. Unlike Thirteen, I didn't have a head injury, or major surgery, or severe physical trauma.

When the jogging is over, just before Carter releases the shock belt from me, she leans forward and says, "See how well we do when we work together?"

I fight the anger that I feel from her sickeningly sweet smile with my new realization: my rehab isn't about my body, it is about my mind. Carter is teaching me to control my urges. To follow orders, even under the stress of my life being held in her hands. She is training me to be obedient. She is teaching me that, if I am to survive here, I need to do as I am told.

Of course, this bothers me, but what upsets me more than what Carter is doing are the possible reasons why she is doing it. As far as everyone here knows, my only disobedience was going off on that aerial drone with Ryan and Jackie and Ten. Is that why I am in "rehab"? If so, why isn't Ten receiving some sort of obedience training as well? Maybe he already did, while I was away. Or maybe they determined that I was the ringleader for that mission and Ten followed because he cared for me. Or—the worst possibility of all—maybe they have figured out that I have been disobedient in other ways.

Could they know about my switch with Six, or my baby, or my plans to find out the truth about this place? Is this how they're trying to stop me?

All I know is that I can't let them stop me. I need to make them think that I am learning my lesson. That I am striving to be exactly the kind of warrior they want. Someone who follows orders rather than her own thoughts about what is right and wrong. A blindly obedient warrior.

Of course, that is something that I will never be.

TUESDAY, JUNE 28
0750

SIX

I've finished telling Nine my story. I've told him everything of importance that I remember about Up There. He listened calmly and quietly, his face full of understanding and compassion. He did exactly as I needed.

"I had a dream about Jose the other night," I add softly. "I feel like I can't let him go." I close my eyes and lean back on the couch, clutching a sleeping Fifty-two. Feeling drained and exhausted.

Without warning, Nine grasps my free hand. My pulse races with anxiety. I open my eyes, searching his, uncertain of his intentions, trying to gather more information, until he lays my palm flat on the center of my chest and presses it there, firm enough that I can feel my quick heartbeat through my jumpsuit.

"Did you love him?" Nine asks softly.

I close my eyes again and search the deepest recesses

of my brain for the answer. And somehow, this time, I find it. For the first time since I awoke from my memory wipe, I think I know how I felt about Jose, after my memories fade away. "I think I cared very deeply for him. But not in the way a woman is supposed to love the man she is paired with. I think I loved him in the way I'm starting to love you." My eyes snap open, worried about how my words have affected Nine. I accidentally admitted an awful truth. That I don't love Nine the way I'm supposed to. True, he must already know that but—

"I love you that way too," he says.

"But we're paired," I say. "We're supposed to be a family."

"We *are* a family," he says.

Nine's hand is still over mine, on my chest, but I feel my body relax.

I suppose that someday Nine's feelings will change. He will want more from me. But it appears that, at this moment, he is satisfied with what we have. We are on the same page, maybe even of the same book.

I pull him into an embrace and allow myself to feel comfort there. Nine is right. We *are* a family. Not the kind of family we're supposed to be. Not the kind of the family the Decision Makers want us to be. We are the kind of family that *we* want to be.

And maybe that is okay.

TUESDAY, JUNE 28
0802

SEVEN

I meet up with my classmates as they head to the underwater classroom for our morning lecture. Twelve catches my eye and gives me a nasty look. If I didn't know that he might be aware of my deepest, most dangerous secret, it'd be almost reassuring to see that he's back to his old obnoxious self. I guess it makes things feel normal, which they most certainly aren't.

I search for Ten, but don't see him. Anxiety rises in my stomach. I make my way over to Twenty-two. "Where's Ten?" I ask him.

"He stayed late to speak with Lieutenant Davis," Twenty-two says.

My heart speeds. *Why would Jackie keep Ten after PT?*

"Did he get in trouble?" I ask.

Twenty-two shakes his head. "She said she had a quick

question for him."

That sounds benign.

Suddenly, a long, high-pitched beep comes from my navigator, sending my heart into my throat. But it isn't just *my* navigator that's beeping. Everyone's wrist is sounding an alarm.

All eyes focus on their screens as words begin to scroll across them:

This is a test of the emergency alert system.

This is only a test.

As the screen fills with zeros and ones, people return to their quiet chatting. I turn to Nineteen and Twenty-two. "Have the navigators done that before?" I ask them. This didn't happen during the first three months that I was here, but I missed the nine months after that.

"They test the emergency system every couple of months," Nineteen says. "My instructor told me that, in an actual emergency, there would be information on the screen about what we should do."

"With all that's been happening lately, it's a good thing they're making sure it's working," Twenty-two says.

Nineteen nods her agreement, and I offer an uneasy smile, pretending to concur. I haven't shared my concerns about this place with anyone other than Ten yet. Ten and I share the same gut feelings, but in order to convince others that something sinister is going on, if in fact it is, we're going to need proof. If all goes as we have planned, we will have that proof before long.

I just hope we get it before it's too late.

TUESDAY, JUNE 28
0810

TEN

Jackie walks alongside me under the pretense of escorting me to class. So far, our conversation has centered on small talk, but I can tell that there's something that's upsetting her. We're nearly at the stairway that leads down to the underwater classroom, when she guides me into the small white room where we planned our secret missions months ago. She scans the door shut behind us.

"I need your help," she says in a low voice.

"Okay," I say, recalling the times that Jackie risked her own safety to help Seven and me.

"I'm wondering if you might be able to poke around on your tablet and see if you can locate the personnel files," she says. "Of course they're classified, so they'll be fairly hidden, but I have the filename."

Jackie doesn't know that I've been poring over classified files for months. I haven't come across any personnel files, but all of the filenames and their contents are encrypted and so it's only by trial and error that I've found files of interest. There are many that I still haven't explored.

"What's the name?" I ask.

"POINT underscore DUME underscore ASSETS. The words are in all caps, I think," she says.

"All right," I say. "And if I can find them, then what?"

"I need you to open the file for David Erikson. He's the soldier who was taken down on the beach yesterday morning. I need to know why."

I feel a spark of interest. I too want to know the soldier's crime, mostly so that Seven and I can be sure to avoid a similar one. But even if the information she was seeking was of no importance to me, I'd still do as Jackie asked. She put her life at risk for Seven and me. I owe her this.

"I'll do my best," I assure her.

And I will.

TUESDAY, JUNE 28
1840

JACKIE

I choke down my dinner, trying to act as normal as possible as conversation swirls around me regarding yesterday's events.

"It's about time we obliterated that Outsider base," one of the soldiers says between mouthfuls.

"I don't know why the hell it took us so long," a second soldier adds. "Should've wiped them off the planet twenty years ago, right after the Great Warrior Massacre."

Anger rises into my throat as my ears fill with a chorus of unanimous agreement. The only thing that keeps me from lashing out is that these soldiers don't know the truth. They don't know that, up until early yesterday morning, every one of those warriors who supposedly died in the Great Warrior Massacre was actually alive and living free in our compound. These soldiers have no idea how many innocent people perished in the military's attack.

When the personnel here at the base were briefed about the destruction of the Outsider compound, the details about the loss of life were minimized. The way the information was presented, you would have thought that the only people harmed in the incident were those directly responsible for the past attacks on the military.

Those of us who visited the site of the destruction and saw the wreckage for ourselves aren't allowed to discuss what we witnessed because our mission was classified. But even those who visited the site surely don't understand the true extent of what the military did. They didn't see the bodies of the dead.

I look over at Lieutenant Commander Wong, careful not to catch her eye. She is focused on her meal, but I can tell she's listening to the conversation. She seems strangely unaffected by it. I wonder how much she knows about the mission. Was she involved in the planning and execution of the murder of my people? Does she know that the Outsider compound was mostly a home for families who were just trying to survive?

It is a chore to finish my meal. The food sits in my stomach like a rock. As soon as I swallow the last bite, I head to my quarters where I activate my tablet and open the secret communication center. My spirit plummets even further when I find no new messages. Maybe my reply to yesterday's message was somehow lost. I send a duplicate, just in case. Then I stare at the screen, willing the survivors to receive my transmission. To respond. To let me know they're still out there.

To let me know they're still alive.

TUESDAY, JUNE 28
1920

SIX

After dinner, I go to the plaza garden with Nine, Three, and Four, along with our babies. Three and Four's child is two weeks older than Fifty-two. He is a striking infant. He has Three's dark skin and black hair, and he has Four's light-brown eyes. He's quite handsome really. I have a feeling that baby Fifty-two agrees with my assessment. When the children are face to face, she always stares at him, appearing utterly fascinated. Sometimes she smiles, sometimes she only stares. Tonight, she's just staring. He's staring at her as well.

Three and I are careful to hold the babies far enough apart that they can't touch. Although of course infants wouldn't be punished for touching each other, the adults who permitted it would be.

"They'll probably be best friends when they're older," Four says, noting the children's enthrallment with each other.

"I'm sure they will," Three says. "Children tend to be friends if their parents are friends."

"I suppose if their parents' personalities are compatible then so are the children's," Nine offers.

I give Nine a smile. I finally feel somewhat comfortable around him. Like we really are a pair, even though we don't act like one when we are alone together in our bedroom capsule. Nine and I still have our secrets though. He doesn't know that I love Three in a way that I'm not supposed to. He has no idea that, last night, she and I took off our clothes and did what can almost be described as mating.

Three's gaze meets mine. "Do you want to go for a walk?" she asks me. "I was hoping to continue our conversation from last night."

As much as I am looking forward to another private meeting with Three, Nine and I already made plans. Even if we hadn't, I can't abandon him tonight, especially after how he supported me this morning. "I'm sorry," I say. "Nine and I were planning to play chess this evening."

Nine gives me an easy smile. "I have a lot of reading to do for work. Would you mind pushing our game to tomorrow?"

"I'd hate to miss it," I say, unwilling to desert him.

"Why don't we *all* go play chess?" Four suggests. "We

could play a lightning game, in teams, and then the girls could go on their walk."

"A quick game would be nice," Nine agrees.

"Great!" Three says, flashing a grin.

And so Nine, Three, Four, and I go off to play chess, my body tingling with anticipation of what might come next.

TUESDAY, JUNE 28
1930

TEN

Seven and I skip the evening movie again tonight. We have much more important things to do. When we arrive at her quarters, I access the classified files on my tablet and set the decryptor to search for POINT_DUME_ASSETS. Once the program is hunting for Jackie's files, I open the map of the warrior compound and settle down on the bed next to Seven to study it with her.

The warrior compound is made up of twenty matching units, each consisting of a dining room, a recreation room, and a collection of quarters. Enlisted Quarters are on the first level and Officers' Quarters are underwater. Each pair of units shares eight common gymnasiums and a large underwater conference room. In the center of the compound is a hub where the hospital and administrative offices are located.

Seven's finger traces the various hallways, checking

the number of occupants in each room. "After you were rescued, did they give you any special therapy to try to convince you to be obedient?" she asks me as she explores.

"Not that I'm aware of," I say. "Why do you ask?"

"Because I'm beginning to think that my rehabilitation isn't about physical therapy," she says. "I think they're trying to manipulate me psychologically. Trying to teach me to be obedient."

"How are they doing that?" I ask.

"They're ensuring that I follow every instruction exactly." She inhales and looks away. "If not, I'm punished."

"You mean like the 'therapy' they gave us in training?" I ask, trying to understand.

"Like that," she says, "only worse."

I feel my body tense with anger. "What exactly are they doing to you?" I ask.

Her eyes remain focused on the map. She is quiet for almost a minute before she finally speaks, "The first day, my therapist put me on a treadmill. She told me to keep pace with it. When I went too fast, she gave me a shock so strong I couldn't stand up. I could hardly think."

I clench my jaw to keep my response controlled. "What else?" I ask, holding my voice steady.

"Today, she put me in some sort of bubble and compressed me so hard that I could barely move, barely breathe. I was completely at her mercy. At the end of the session, she smiled at me and said that things go better when I cooperate."

"Did she say what would happen if you didn't?" I ask.

"She didn't have to. If I was disobedient enough, I don't think she'd hesitate to ..." She turns her face toward me. There's resignation there.

I inhale, holding back the urge to react with fury. "Maybe we should talk to the commander," I suggest.

She shakes her head. "For all we know, he's the one who ordered this."

She's right. The commander was aware of the "therapy" we received during training and he allowed it. He surely wants us to be obedient and not cause trouble. Maybe this is his way of ensuring Seven's cooperation.

"I think exploring the compound is a bad idea," I say. If they are concerned with Seven's obedience, poking around the compound is far too risky.

She locks her eyes with mine. "We have to. Things aren't right here. We need to find out the truth. We need to fix things, so we can make life better for the people back home. For our daughter."

Seven's eyes can convince me of anything, even things that are unwise. "Then we need to be smart about it," I acquiesce. "Plan it like Ryan taught us. With worst-case scenarios. Like a mission."

Seven smiles. "Okay."

I return my focus to the map. "We should probably start with someplace where we're unlikely to be caught." I zoom in on some officers' quarters on the underwater level. "Maybe here."

"Officers' quarters?" she asks, with a hint of skepticism.

"I've been monitoring them for weeks. They've been unoccupied the whole time, along with the enlisted quarters above them."

Seven nods. "All right then. Tomorrow night, we explore the abandoned officers' quarters."

As we begin to plan our mission, my tablet lets out a soft bleep. I click to the search screen and see a folder with the filename Jackie asked me to search for. "It found it!"

"Found what?" Seven asks.

As I open the folder and start the process of decrypting its contents, I tell Seven about the request Jackie made of me, to find information about the soldier who was taken away so roughly yesterday morning.

"Why do you think she wants to know about him so badly?" Seven asks.

"Maybe he was a friend of hers," I say. "Or maybe, like the rest of us, she doesn't want to fall victim to the same fate. Whatever the reason, after all she did for us, I have to help her."

"Of course," Seven agrees.

My tablet beeps again. The screen is now filled with a list of individual filenames. I perform a search for "Erikson."

There is only one. Erikson, David.

I click the file open and, almost immediately, I feel uncomfortable reading it. The information here isn't just impersonal facts. The file tells his story. His likes and dislikes: foods, activities, people. What makes him cry. What makes him scared. His strengths and weaknesses. How he goes about solving problems. Then there are the major events since his arrival. Missions he's participated in. His promotion to Lieutenant. But there's nothing that looks concerning until the last entry, from yesterday:

Terminal Transfer. Reason: Spy.

"The military took him prisoner and destroyed the Outsider compound on the same day," Seven says. "Do you think he was an Outsider?"

"You think there was an Outsider living among us in plain sight?" I ask.

"Sometimes being in plain sight is easier than trying to hide," she says.

"Let's look at some other files." I close Erikson's file and run another search, for Jackie.

Her file is just as unassuming as Erikson's. And the information is just as personal. Why would the military care that Jackie likes the color green better than pink? Why would they care that she enjoys the smell of peaches? Why would they need to know that the first boy she ever kissed was named Ray?

Jackie has no negative notes on her file until nine months ago, when her participation in our covert mission to get Seven back to our home compound was noted. According to the file, she was absolved of guilt. Apparently, Ryan took the blame for the mission. He told the commander that he led Jackie to believe that Seven and I were authorized to be aboard that aerial drone for a top secret operation. Jackie was not punished in any way.

"I guess Ryan took all the punishment," Seven says, her voice tight.

I close Jackie's file and run another search, for Ryan's.

The file for "Ryan, Evan" comes up immediately. I tap it open.

His file is much longer than Jackie's, which makes sense because he has been here for more years. It begins with his entry into the warrior program. Like Jackie, he had no incidents until our unauthorized mission. As noted in Jackie's file, Ryan took responsibility. His file notes that "Significant Negative Reinforcement" was administered.

"What do you think they did to him?" Seven asks, her

eyes brimming with tears.

"Maybe something like isolation back home," I say. Although I imagine that it was probably much worse.

"I want to see Ma'am's file," Seven says.

Looking at the file of her dead instructor may be difficult for Seven, but we should probably see it. "Her name was Anna, right?" I ask.

"Anna Kitay," Seven says.

I run a search and pull up the file that results. The number of negative notes is remarkable. Ma'am always seemed quite controlled and compliant. I never would have guessed that she broke so many rules back when she was a warrior. We scroll through her many infractions—talking back to her instructors, attempting to access restricted areas, refusing to follow orders—and then there is a prominent note:

AMBUSHED BY OUTSIDER TRIBE 28.
ESCAPED CAPTURE.
INDUCED RETROGRADE AMNESIA
ADMINISTERED.

After that, her infractions nearly cease. Something changed her, although it isn't clear what. Her only recent negative note is:

MATERNAL FEELINGS TOWARD WARRIOR
MURPHY.
ACTION TAKEN: REMEDIATION.

"They punished her for feeling motherly toward me?" Seven asks, her voice shaking.

"I doubt the punishment had any effect on her feelings," I say.

"They shouldn't have punished her," Seven says.

At the end of Ma'am's file, her death is noted. Seven stares at the final entry for a minute before she asks, "Are there files for us?"

I close Ma'am's file and search "Hanson."

No results found.

I try "Murphy."

No results found.

I try "Two Thousand Ten" and "Two Thousand Seven" and also just "Ten" and "Seven," but there are no files.

"Search for 'Carter,'" Seven asks.

I do, but again there's no file found. "Who is Carter?" I ask Seven.

"She's my physical therapist."

I stiffen at the thought of the person who is abusing Seven. "The support staff files and warrior files must be in another folder," I say, trying to distract myself from my anger.

"What about 'Johnson'?" Seven asks.

As I type the name into the search box, I ask, "Who's Johnson?"

"The psychiatrist who saw me in rehab," she says. "At least, I think she was a psychiatrist."

"Did she hurt you too?" I ask.

"No."

The name "Johnson, Karen" pops up on the screen.

"That's her," Seven says.

I click open the file. According to the information, Johnson is a doctor of psychiatry who has worked at the base for ten years. All sorts of personal information is listed, but Seven doesn't seem interested in any of that. "What about the commander?" she asks.

I type "Duncan" into the search box. No results are returned.

"The commander's file must be too important to keep with the others," Seven says. "And our files are probably separate because we're warriors. But why wouldn't Carter have a file in here?"

I shake my head. "Maybe she's more important than

she appears."

Seven's mind seems to have already moved on to another thought. "We need to find *our* files," she says. "We need to know what the military knows about us."

"That isn't going to be easy," I say. "There are thousands of encrypted classified files and without a filename, finding the warrior files could be nearly impossible. But I'm going to try."

And so I settle in for a sleepless night.

TUESDAY, JUNE 28
2014

SIX

After our chess game, the boys take the babies back to our domiciles and Three and I head off for our walk. Our destination is unspoken, but we end up at the entrance to the restricted hallways. I pull the tag from underneath my jumpsuit and scan us inside.

I am trembling with excitement by the time we enter the drone closet. Three pulls me into her arms and holds me tight, but I sense there's something bothering her. After a few minutes, she separates from me and goes to sit against the wall.

I take a seat beside her. "What's wrong?" I ask.

Her gaze remains fixed on the floor. "Have you and Nine started mating again?"

My body shivers with discomfort at the thought. "No. We only mated before I left. When we were trying to become pregnant."

"It's okay if you do, you know," she says, looking up at me. "They told us to mate with our partners at least twice per week—"

"But we already have a baby." I was under the impression that mating was only for the purpose of producing offspring.

"We were supposed to resume mating four weeks after the birth of our child," she says. "Didn't your sister tell you that?"

"No." She didn't. "Who told you that we're supposed to keep mating?"

"There was an instructional video after we came home with the baby, about how to maintain a healthy pairing," she says.

And, suddenly, an unpleasant thought leaps into my mind. "Have you been mating with Four?" I ask.

Her gaze falls back to the ground. "We did last night. It was the first time since before I found out I was pregnant."

I swallow, trying to figure out how I feel about her revelation.

Three continues, "Four really enjoys mating. He's held off so long that …"

"It's okay. I understand," I say. And I do understand. I know that someday I will have to mate with Nine again. But I don't feel ready to do that yet.

"I think after you and I … well … you and I kind of mated last night … I guess I feel more comfortable doing what I'm required to do with my pair," she says. "I'm sorry, Six."

I take her back into my arms. "Don't be sorry."

"I wish we could have been paired with each other," she murmurs. "Things would be so much easier that way."

"That isn't how things work here," I say. "Here, everything is easy until you start asking yourself what you really want. Until you start thinking about making your own choices."

"The only choice I care about making is to be with you," Three says.

"I want to be with you too," I whisper.

My hand goes to the zipper of her jumpsuit and I ease it down. Slowly, we remove every bit of our clothes, and we look at each other's bodies in a way that is absolutely forbidden. Completely undressed. I didn't really look at her much last night. We were too busy touching and feeling. Her body is like mine, but yet different. Her curves. The texture of the hair between her legs. Her breasts …

We lie down together on the cold hard floor and share the heat of our bodies once again. For a few fleeting moments, I don't worry about rules and expectations and what is forbidden and what is required. I do what feels right, rather than what is allowed. Wishing these moments could be infinite.

    Knowing that they aren't.

WEDNESDAY, JUNE 29
0656

TEN

It's difficult to watch Seven go off to rehab now that I know what awaits her there. I walk her all the way to the door, but I can't accompany her inside and that physically hurts.

"I'll be okay," Seven says. Sometimes she can read the thoughts right off my face.

"I know you will." Unlike Seven, I don't believe that Carter would seriously harm her for disobedience. It would raise too many questions if she became injured during routine rehab. I know Seven can handle whatever else is about to happen, but that doesn't make this any easier.

I press my palm to hers, they way we've done ever since we were very young. And then, I turn and go. Just before I round the corner, I glance back and see Seven take a deep breath, and activate the greeter at the door.

I arrive one minute late for PT. As I enter the

gymnasium, Jackie catches my gaze, but her expression isn't one of reproach. She is asking a question.

I give her a nod. *Yes, I found what you asked.*

She exhales.

Once PT is over, I let my friends go off ahead to class and I wait for Jackie. After everyone has left the gymnasium, she approaches me. "May I walk with you to class?" she asks.

I nod, knowing full-well that we're not going straight to class.

As anticipated, Jackie leads me to the little white room. Once she scans the door closed behind us, I pull my tablet from my pocket and unfold it.

"I found most of the personnel files," I say as I bring up Erikson's file.

Jackie pores over its contents, appearing intensely interested in what is there, almost peculiarly so. When she finishes, she looks seriously disturbed.

"What's 'Terminal Transfer'?" I ask, referring to the final entry on the file.

"It's a place where people are sent to live out their lives in solitary confinement." She sighs uncomfortably. "But I have a sneaking suspicion that prisoners don't live very long there. What good does it do to keep an unwanted prisoner alive?"

"Who do you think Erikson was spying for?" I ask.

"I don't know." Her gaze drops back to the tablet. "How did you access the file?"

I hesitate. Showing Jackie how I access the classified files is probably not a good idea. But I owe her a debt that I will likely never be able to repay. And so, step by step, I demonstrate how I bypassed the tablet's security features.

"It's clear why they chose you to be a warrior," she says when I'm through.

"How do you think they chose the warriors?" I ask.

"They select people who think outside the box," she says. "Who aren't just smart, but are imaginative, inventive, resourceful. You and Murphy are exactly the kind of warriors they look for."

"But we don't do as we're told," I say. "I doubt that's something they look for."

She gives the smallest of smiles. "I suppose not. But you're going to do great things for the program ... for the world. If they didn't think so, they'd send you to Terminal Transfer too." Even though her statement sounds like a threat, I can tell that she means it as a warning, inspired by her desire to keep Seven and me safe. "You'd best be going," she adds. "You're going to be late for class."

"Right," I say. I fold my tablet and slip it back into my pocket.

Just before Jackie scans open the door, she turns to me. "Be careful, Hanson."

I give her a smile. "You be careful too," I say.

Jackie looks at me the same way my mother did right before I left for The War. A mix of respect and worry. Then she scans the door open and then closed behind us, and she disappears around the corner.

WEDNESDAY, JUNE 29
1813

SIX

After work, I pick up Fifty-two at Infant Stim, but I'm in no rush to go to dinner. For one thing, I'm not hungry at all and for another, I'm still trying to figure out how I feel about Three mating with Four. And so, instead of going directly to my assigned restaurant for this evening, I go down to the plaza garden and sit by the fish tank. Seven told me that watching the fish helps her figure out her thoughts. Maybe it will work for me too.

I focus on a small silver fish near the bottom of the tank. As he slowly makes his way past the tall stacks of gray rocks, I let my thoughts drift along with him.

Three is mating with Four again. That bothers me, even though maybe it shouldn't. Three said it is required for pairs to mate twice per week, even after their pregnancy window has closed. That's why she did it. That and the fact that Four really wanted to.

I wonder if Nine wants to mate with me. I guess he

thinks that I am unaware that we are supposed to be mating—since I missed the post-childbirth instructional video—and he's too shy to suggest it. If we don't discuss it, then we could go on not mating until it is time for us to get pregnant again. In ten years. But if Nine wants us to mate in the interim, is it fair to deny him that?

I've mated with Nine before, and so I know it isn't particularly frightening or painful. The main thing that used to bother me about it was that I felt forced to mate. Required to do something that felt wrong to me. Or, more correctly, to do something that might have felt right if I were doing it with a different person.

I guess there are lots of things that I am forced to do in my life. I am forced to awaken at the required time, and go to work, and eat my meals in their entireties, and report for whatever examinations, evaluations, or activities are scheduled for me. My entire life has been decided for me, but being forced to mate is one of the very few decisions that have felt wrong to me.

As I stare at the little fish, who has now reached the end of the tank and has turned back the way he came, I realize what I must do. I chose to live here, rather than above the sky. And so I must maintain the appearance of being a cooperative member of the community. I must keep my forbidden thoughts quiet and my forbidden actions hidden. I will allow myself to have them, but I must not let anyone else know that I have enough secrets for a lifetime.

And I must mate with Nine.

WEDNESDAY, JUNE 29
1911

SEVEN

Rehab went better than I expected. Carter seems to think that I've learned my lesson. And so, while our session today was stressful, at least it was not painful. At lunch, Ten and I went back to his quarters and he told me about his meeting with Jackie. He suggested that we tell Ryan about the personnel files, and I agreed. Ryan's experience here might enable him to see something we've missed. And even if not, I want him to have as much information as possible to help ensure his safety.

We meet with Ryan in the little white room, and Ten pulls up the map of the warrior compound on his tablet. He hovers his finger over the room we now occupy. Zero people.

"It doesn't know we're in here," Ten says and then he slides his finger over to the recreation room. "It sees twenty-three people in the rec room."

Ryan peers at the screen. "That's an interesting map."

"You've never seen a map of the compound before?" I ask in disbelief.

"Not one that tells you how many people are in a room," he says. "Where did you find that?"

Ten exhales and I know what he's thinking. He was ambivalent about sharing this information with Jackie. Now he is about to reveal it to someone else. At least both Jackie and Ryan are people we can trust.

"I accessed classified documents," Ten admits. Before Ryan can ask further questions, Ten continues, "I also found some personnel files. I thought you might want to see yours."

Ryan's forehead creases. "Have you already looked at it?"

"Yes," Ten admits.

Ryan takes a few minutes to review his file. "No surprises here," he finally says. "So how did you happen upon these files?"

"Jackie asked me to find the file of the soldier who was taken prisoner yesterday," Ten says.

Ryan's eyes narrow. "Did she say why she was so interested?"

"No," Ten says.

"Maybe she feels that something's not right about it all," I blurt out.

Ryan looks at me. At first, I feel like he's about to admonish me, but then he says, "Well, she'd be correct about that."

My stomach tightens with concern. I guess maybe I was hoping that Ryan would disagree, that he would assure us that everything here is okay. But it's better that he doesn't. I don't think I would trust him if he reassured us.

Ryan's eyes appear tired … exhausted really. The way they did after Ma'am died. "What's wrong?" I ask, afraid to hear the answer. But whatever it is, I'd rather know than not know.

He fixes his gaze on the wall, as if trying to find strength in its emptiness. "From the day your sister and I were taken prisoner, the military knew exactly where we were being held captive. Their search was for appearances only. They never had any intention of recovering us."

Is that possible? Would the military willingly sacrifice their own? I've never known Ryan to lie to me, and so I consider that he believes this to be true. But if it is true, it sickens me in a way that nothing ever has before. How could the people in charge of protecting us forsake us? The Outsiders could have killed Ryan and Six. How could the military have taken no action to save them?

"So that's why the command center was deserted on the night you were found," Ten says.

"They'd made a conscious decision to let us go. When

you saw us on the surveillance drone footage, you forced their hand. They had to rescue us." He exhales. "When I first got back here, I didn't know all that. During the debriefing, I told them everything I knew about the Outsiders. I told them that the nine warriors who were thought to have perished in the Great Warrior Massacre were alive, and they were living at the Outsiders' compound. I told them that I'd been forced to mate with numerous Outsider women, and that I had fathered infants there, as well as offspring who had not yet been born. Yesterday morning, they leveled the Outsiders' compound. They killed hundreds of innocent men, women, and children. They killed their own warriors ..." He swallows, and his gaze falls to the floor.

My head spins horribly with the information Ryan has revealed. *The Great Warrior Massacre warriors were alive? Ryan fathered babies with the Outsiders? The military killed them all?* I knew this was a place of lies and secrets. I knew that something wasn't right here. But never would I have thought that the military would do something that atrocious.

For a moment, my mind leaps back in time, plunging me right into yesterday, standing there in that horrific place, staring at all of the dead bodies, wondering who could do such a terrible thing. Now I have an answer ... us.

"The commander said they did it to protect us," I say.

"Ninety-nine percent of the people they killed yesterday were not a threat." Ryan's voice shakes with anger. "This isn't the way our military is supposed to operate. We don't protect our innocents by destroying the innocents of others. There is no excuse for what we did yesterday. And I won't let anything like this happen again."

"How are you going to stop it?" Ten asks.

I know the answer. I've known it for a long time, even though I wasn't exactly sure what the question was. "We need to tell everyone the truth." But even though this is the answer, and this is what must be done, there are no guarantees that telling people the truth will change things. In fact, revealing the truth could make things worse.

The truth can be dangerous. Especially when it is nearly impossible to believe.

WEDNESDAY, JUNE 29
1923

TEN

Seven and I go back to her quarters. We both agree that, given what Ryan has told us, exploring the compound with my chip is too risky. I set Seven up on her tablet, so she can check for any unusual activity on the compound map, and I get to work decrypting classified files, looking for anything that could be of help.

I am deep in concentration when our navigators let out a high-pitched tone—the one for the test of the emergency alert system. The second test in as many days.

"That's strange," I say as I watch the zeros and ones tick across the navigator's screen. "They don't usually test the system two days in a row."

"Something is definitely wrong here," Seven says.

I am about to return my attention to the classified files, when a thought flickers in my brain, a memory. "Those numbers ..." I start.

"Nineteen said if this was an actual emergency they'd put information on the screen there about what to do," Seven says.

"My great grandfather once taught me that all text can be converted into a series of ones and zeros, using mathematical calculations. It's called binary code. Apparently, the code was used in the early days of technology. No one has talked about it for a long time, except for my great grandfather."

I slip my navigator into record mode until the numbers are done scrolling and the navigator returns to sleep. Then I play them back slowly. There must be hundreds of them. I hand my navigator to Seven and open my homemade decryptor. "Would you read off these numbers?"

She reads from the screen as I type, "One, one, one, zero, zero …"

After we have about fifty numbers, I decide to test it. I click translate, and seemingly-random strings of letters, numbers, and symbols appear on the screen. Meaningless gibberish.

"I guess the numbers could just be placeholders," I say, dissatisfied.

"Maybe we missed something," Seven says.

And then I realize … "Maybe we did." I smile as hope surges into me. "In binary code, information is represented by a *string* of zeros and ones. If I started recording partway through one of the strings, then everything beyond it wouldn't make sense. Maybe I just need to find the beginning of a string."

I delete the first number and translate. In return, I get gibberish. Different from the first gibberish, but gibberish nonetheless. I delete the next number. Gibberish. And the next. Gibberish. And the next …

The gibberish disappears. And *words* appear in its place.

"It *is* a code!" Seven breathes, and then she reads the translation aloud, "Sets are spectacular tog." She looks at me. "But what does it mean?"

"It must mean something," I say.

"Of course it does," she says.

Of course she's right. No one bothers encoding things unless they have something to hide.

WEDNESDAY, JUNE 29
1935

SIX

After dinner, I go straight back to my domicile. I told Three that I needed to spend time with Nine tonight because I changed our plans last night. I haven't told her that I decided to start mating with him again. I didn't want her to have to think about it. Now that she's already given me permission, by her words and actions, it's probably better that I just quietly do what I am supposed to do, maintaining the health of my pairing. Doing as I am required.

When Nine and I enter our domicile, Fifty-two is asleep. Normally I would let her sleep on my chest, but given what Nine and I are about to do, I put her in her safe sleeping space in our gathering room. Then I join Nine on the couch. He passes me my tablet and then focuses his attention on his own.

"Do you have a lot of reading to do again tonight?" I ask.

"No," he says. "I didn't have a lot to read last night either."

"Why did you say that you did?" I ask, even though I'm now certain of the answer. He made an excuse because he could tell that I wanted to go on that walk with Three.

"You needed time with your friend," he says.

I put my hand over his. "You're my friend too."

He averts his gaze. "Not in the same way."

"I want to mate with you," I say quickly.

His eyes look into mine, but they are narrowed with suspicion. "Why?" he asks.

There are many reasons, but I chose just one. "Three told me that we're required to mate twice per week, even now that the baby is here."

"Nobody but us will know whether we do that or not," he says.

"I know," I say. "But don't you want us to mate?"

"No." He inhales, as if he might say something more, but he doesn't continue.

Of course he doesn't want to mate with me. I'm sure the only reason he mated with me in the past was because we needed to get pregnant. Why else would he have done it through all my tears? I wish I could have controlled them. I tried so hard, but no matter what I did, I couldn't hold them back. They came from deep inside me. From my core. They must have made Nine feel absolutely awful. It's no wonder that he doesn't want to mate with me again.

"I promise I won't cry anymore," I say.

"Why did you cry before?" He has asked that question of me many times, but I never gave him an answer.

"I felt like I was being forced. Not by you, but by the Decision Makers. The same people who assigned me to be a warrior. They shouldn't force us to be something we're not."

Nine nods. "I agree."

"But now, like you said, no one will know whether we're mating or not," I say. "So it's our decision."

"And you want us to mate?" he asks.

"I want us to be a healthy pair," I say.

"I want that too." He presses his lips together and then adds, "But I don't want to mate."

"Because of me?" I ask. But it's really more of a statement than a question.

"No," he says, looking directly into my eyes. "Because of me."

"What do you mean?" I ask.

He shifts uncomfortably on the couch. "I never wanted to mate with you, even before the first time we did, because I thought you'd wanted to be paired with Ten."

"That was back when you believed I was Seven," I argue. His explanation doesn't hold true now that he knows who I really am. "What about now?"

"I wanted to be paired with someone else too," he says softly.

"Who?" I ask. It's none of my business, but—

"I wanted to be paired with Thirteen," he says, staring straight ahead. "I thought when she went above the sky, she was going to die. After a few weeks, I figured she must be dead. And we needed to get pregnant. We needed to get on with our lives. That's when I finally mated with you. But Seven told me that Thirteen's alive …"

"She is," I say. "I saw her with my own eyes."

He smiles sadly. "I know it's silly, but I feel like, if she's still alive …" He stops and focuses his attention on me rather than the empty space ahead of him.

"It isn't silly at all," I say.

He shakes his head. "Thirteen and I weren't even friends. I was always too nervous to talk to her. Who knows if she would have liked me? Even if we had been paired together …"

"Any woman would be lucky to be paired with you," I say.

"Not *you* though," he says. "You wanted to be paired with Three."

My heart freezes. *How could he possibly know …?* "Why would you say that?"

"Because I see the way you look at her. It's the same way Seven looked at Ten," he says. "Do you love her?"

161

I swallow. "I do," I say. And then I wait for his reaction. Will it be shock? Confusion? Rejection?

Nine says nothing. Instead, he accepts me into his arms. We don't exchange words, but I don't think we need them right now. I know that Nine understands.

When it is time for sleep, we crawl into our bedroom capsule and I let my body rest close to his. There is nothing to fear with him anymore. He knows all of my secrets. And I think I know all of his. Our life together will never be as we'd hoped it would be, but inside the walls of our domicile, we will be safe with each other, understood.

Maybe that will be good enough.

WEDNESDAY, JUNE 29

1942

SEVEN

Ten and I stare at the rows upon rows of words. A collection of phrases: "rabbits eat carrots blood is red dogs are furry …" Each is a statement of fact, except for one: "Conference Room Twelve," I read aloud.

"I wonder if …" Ten starts, but I am already mentally traveling down the same path, I think, because he stops speaking as soon as I grab my tablet and pull up the compound map.

I hover my finger over Conference Room Twelve. "There are thirty-two people in there," I report to Ten. I check the other conference rooms. Zero. Zero. Zero. Zero … "Conference Room Twelve is the only one that's occupied."

"That can't just be a coincidence," Ten says.

"So the code is an announcement for a secret meeting," I say.

"It must be."

"But what do all the other words mean?" I ask.

"I missed the first hundred or so numbers," he says. "Maybe there was something there that could offer an explanation."

Suddenly, a dialogue box pops up on my tablet. I'd been resting my hand on the screen. *An error message? …* No … It's a question:

Show surveillance view?

My pulse races with hesitant excitement. There are two options: yes and no.

I choose yes.

Little red dots immediately populate the map. They're everywhere. In hallways. In rooms. I hover my finger over one and a video image appears above the screen. It shows the inside of a hallway. Two soldiers stroll down the corridor, chatting.

"The red spots are security cameras!" Ten says.

The soldiers round a corner, disappearing from the video image. I hover over the red dot in the connecting hallway and see the same soldiers again.

"Open a camera in the conference room," Ten suggests.

I hover my finger over one of the red dots in the conference room and a rectangular red box pops up with a message:

Video unavailable.

I try another camera in the room. And then another.

The video from all of the cameras in the conference room is unavailable.

"There's something going on in that room that they don't want anyone to know about," Ten says.

I hover my finger over the red dot in the stairwell outside the conference room and an image pops up. The stairwell is empty, for now. "We can't see what's going on inside the room," I say. "But at least we can see who comes out."

Ten smiles. "So now we wait." He pulls up the map on his own tablet. "How did you access the security footage?" he asks me.

"I think ... I'm not sure but ... I was resting my hand on the screen," I say.

Ten passes me his tablet. "Do exactly what you did."

I place my hand on the screen, trying to do it the same way as before. Nothing happens.

And then, just before I lift my hand to try again, a message appears:

Show surveillance view?

"Press and hold on the border," Ten murmurs as he shakes his head. "I thought I'd tried everything. But I didn't try that."

"Now we can explore the compound without risk," I say, a grin spreading across my face. "We can go anywhere the cameras are."

"And there are *hundreds* of them," Ten says.

For the first time in a long time, I see the Ten who I knew long ago. The Ten who took me into forbidden places. The Ten who encouraged me to be inquisitive. To question things. To think for myself rather than let my thoughts be governed by others.

I look into his curious eyes, and smile back. "Where do you want to start?"

WEDNESDAY, JUNE 29
1947

TEN

It is as if Seven and I are invisible. Able to poke around the warrior compound, passing like ghosts through doors to see what's on the other side. I zoom in on our current location. The girls' quarters. I am relieved to see that there are no cameras in the individual rooms. Only in the hallway.

I start our journey there. Imagining that we are wandering down the hallway. Happening upon people who are unaware that we're traveling vicariously beside them. We take a quick look inside the rec room. A few of our classmates are there, watching a movie. No one is in the dining room. I head back into the hallway, traveling toward the abandoned officers' quarters, the first place I'd planned to explore.

When I first discovered the compound map and learned that there were quarters located under the water, I imagined what it would be like to live there. The underwater conference room has always been my favorite room in the warrior compound, because being inside it is like being in the center of a huge fish tank. To have my quarters inside a fish tank too would be amazing.

My imagination did not prepare me for what I see as I open the video from the stairwell that leads to the officers' quarters. The walls are transparent. My excitement builds as I visualize myself descending the black stairs into the depths of the ocean. The next camera takes us into a hallway. Like in the stairwell, the hallway walls provide an inside look at the ocean. Fish shimmer in the dimming water. In the daytime, this hallway must be absolutely spectacular.

"It's incredible down there," Seven breathes.

I nod in agreement.

The hallway branches into two corridors that lead to the individual quarters. The doors to the quarters are all open. There are no cameras inside the individual rooms, but one of the hallway cameras allows us a glimpse through an open door. The room is simple. A bed. A desk. A chair. A small attached space that contains a toilet, sink, and shower. But the walls, along with the ceiling and floor, are transparent. Kelp dances outside. An orange fish darts under the floor.

"If I lived there, I'd just sit and stare at the fish all day long," Seven says.

I laugh—the first time I've laughed in a long time. "I would too."

We tear ourselves away from the officers' quarters, because there's so much left to explore. After a quick glance at Seven's tablet, which still shows video of the empty stairwell outside Conference Room Twelve, we move on to the abandoned enlisted quarters, deciding to proceed systematically through the compound.

As expected, the hallway is empty. As is the dining room. But when I hover my finger over one of the small red dots in the recreation room, the video that appears is puzzling. There are *people* there. Nine people. I've checked the number of occupants in this area many times over the past few months, and each time, the entire place was empty.

"I thought you said these quarters were unoccupied," Seven says.

"They were," I say. "Every time I looked."

I press and hold the border of the map—which, as I suspected, switches me back to the original view of the map—and I hover my finger over the same rec room.

"Zero," Seven reads off the screen. "The map isn't picking up what's going on in there."

"It could be a malfunction," I say, clicking back to the surveillance view, "but I doubt that."

I zoom in and notice that every person in the room is wearing a white jumpsuit. "Have you ever seen anyone wear a white jumpsuit here?" I ask Seven.

"No," she says. "Only the children back home."

I check every face. These people are adults, but I don't recognize any of them.

"Maybe they're custodial robots or something," Seven suggests. "Maybe robots don't show up on the occupancy count."

I nod. "That could be."

"We'll have to keep an eye on them," she says. "See what they do."

"Right …" I say, but before I continue, I am distracted by the screen of Seven's tablet. I focus on it just in time to see the video image that, moments ago, showed the stairwell outside Conference Room Twelve go black.

WEDNESDAY, JUNE 29
1955

SEVEN

"What happened to the video?" Ten asks, directing my attention to the screen of my tablet. The image from the stairwell camera outside Conference Room Twelve is now gone. "Did it time out or something?"

I hover my finger over another red spot on the map a distance away. An image of an empty gymnasium pops up, but when I go back to the conference room stairwell, I get an error message:

Video unavailable.

I try a camera in the conference room.

Video unavailable.

I try other cameras one by one, moving out from the

conference room each time. It isn't until we are a few hallways away that we get an image. A few soldiers are walking down the corridor, but it's impossible to tell whether they're coming from the conference room or someplace else.

"So much for finding out who attended the meeting," I sigh. "Even if we were to go there physically now, we'd be too late."

"We'll have to wait for the next one," Ten says. "If there is a next one."

A familiar face passes into the image. "That's Carter!" I exclaim.

Ten zooms in on her face. "Your physical therapist?"

"Yes." Carter begins a conversation with someone who has come up beside her. "Who's she talking to?" I ask Ten.

He zooms the image back out, and my blood turns cold as I see the answer. "She's talking to the commander," I say. Carter laughs, apparently in response to something he has said.

"It looks like the two of them are well acquainted," Ten remarks.

And then I have another chilling thought. "They're coming from the direction of the conference room. Do you think they were part of the secret meeting?"

"I'm guessing that the commander is the one who

called the meeting," Ten says. "If Carter was one of only thirty-two people in attendance, she must be important to whatever they were discussing." He takes my hand firmly, protectively. "You need to be extremely careful around her. If she's on the commander's side, and we're right about what's going here, then she's dangerous. Just like the commander himself."

I hate to think of the commander as dangerous. He's big and imposing, and at first he frightened me, but after I got to know him a little, I got the feeling that he was on our side. If he ordered Carter to teach me to be obedient, couldn't he have thought he was doing it for my own good? If he ordered an attack on the Outsider's compound, couldn't he have felt that it was the only way to ensure our protection?

Yes, I suppose all of that could be true. But deep in my gut, deep down inside me, I don't trust him anymore. I don't trust any of those in charge. Ten is right, I must be ready to be attacked at any time. Because, whether or not those in charge know it yet, Ten and I are a potential threat to them. And they will surely waste no time in destroying us once they figure that out.

THURSDAY, JUNE 30
0535

TEN

I wake up before the morning alarm and find Seven
sitting at her desk, working on her tablet. When she notices
that I'm awake, she joins me in bed. "They're still in the rec
room," she says. Even without looking at the screen, I know
she's referring to the people—or robots—in the white
jumpsuits who we discovered yesterday in the abandoned
enlisted quarters.

"Not all of them," she continues. "I guess some are
still asleep. I think they sleep in the individual quarters. I
saw a woman coming out of one of the rooms about fifteen
minutes ago and a man coming from a different room a few
minutes later."

"Robots don't sleep," I say.

"Robots don't drink either," she says, zooming in on
the tanks along the rec room wall. In our rec room, the
tanks are filled with colored liquids that muddle people's

minds, but these tanks are filled only with clear liquid—water, I suppose. "I saw a few of them drinking."

"So there are *people* here who we've never seen, even though they share common gymnasiums with us, who don't show up on the map as occupants of the rooms they occupy," I say.

"We need to show this to Ryan," Seven says.

Without a word, I agree.

THURSDAY, JUNE 30

0655

SEVEN

After a quiet breakfast, Ten walks me to the rehab unit and says a tense goodbye. I activate the greeter and Carter welcomes me inside. She leads me to the pod.

"How are you doing today?" she asks as if we are friends getting together for a social chat.

"I'm fine," I reply, careful to match my tone with my words. "How are you?"

"Excellent." The enthusiasm with which she says it makes me wince.

"Undress and climb aboard," she says, gesturing to the purple pod.

She's never been this informal with me before, but it is normal for healthcare providers to be relaxed, even joke with their patients, once they've gotten to know each other. Generally, it puts the patient at ease and improves rapport. But there is nothing that Carter could say or do that could enhance my bond with her.

Still, I must act engaged. I give her a smile as I settle into the pod.

The monitoring wires and mask are attached and the pod grips hold of me.

"Ready for stretches?" Carter asks.

"Yes," I say, willing my body to relax.

"Great, let's begin."

As before, the pod starts its regimen with my feet. It brings my feet into the tiptoe position but, just when I think it has found my limit, it goes further, enough that it hurts.

"Try to relax," Carter says pleasantly.

I *did* tense up, but only because of the unexpected discomfort. I force myself to relax, but instead of letting up, the pod takes my joint further past its limit.

I gasp, biting my lip to keep myself from crying out in pain.

"Relax," Carter says. And the pod pushes my joint further.

"I can't," I force out. My body is instinctively fighting the pod. Defending itself from being broken.

"Is this too much for you to handle?" Carter asks, far too amiably considering what she is making the pod do to me.

Tears form in my eyes from the pain that's now seizing the arches of my feet. "Yes," I say. "It's too much."

"All right," she says.

The pod brings my feet to their neutral position. As the pain eases, I exhale.

Carter looks into my tear-filled eyes without even a hint of empathy.

"Did I do something wrong?" I ask her.

"I'm just trying to help you, Murphy," she says. "Are you ready to continue?"

"Do I have a choice?" I ask.

"Of course not," she says, without breaking her stare.

It's clear that Carter will proceed with or without my permission. And so I grant her the permission to continue her torture of me. I try to distract myself by attempting to reason out why she is hurting me. After our relatively easy session yesterday, I thought I'd convinced Carter that she'd accomplished her goal. And so far today, I thought I'd been nothing but obedient. I arrived on time and followed all of her instructions without argument. So why is she hurting me? Why is she pushing me past my limits? The only answer I can come up with is that she is trying to break me. Not physically. She is trying to break my spirit.

Although I don't know for certain why I am being punished, I know one thing. As long as I am living, no one will break me. Not Carter. Not the commander. I can handle whatever they do to me.

My muscles and joints ache. My eyes grow wetter and

wetter from the tears I can't control. My arms and legs shake with adrenaline released by my body even though I will it not to. But I don't break. Because I am brave. I am strong.

I am a warrior.

THURSDAY, JUNE 30
1216

TEN

After a quick lunch, Seven, Ryan, and I settle down in the small white room that has seen so many of our clandestine activities. "How are you so sure they're not monitoring us here?" I ask Ryan. After Seven discovered the surveillance view on the compound map, I checked to see if there were cameras in this room. There were not. I also noted that the hallway cameras in the vicinity don't show the room's entrance. Still, I wonder what information Ryan has about it.

"This room is unmonitored. It's meant for classified discussions. Just in case, I use a signal interrupter whenever we're in here." He pulls up a screen on his navigator and I see an unusual tracing that weaves up and down erratically.

"Does the commander know you have that?" Seven asks.

"No," he says. "I don't think he'd be too happy about

it."

"Where'd you get it?" I ask.

"I constructed it myself," he says.

I wish I could ask him to show me how he did it, but we don't have the luxury of much time right now. Seven and I need to tell him what we've found. I pull up the phrases that I translated from the last emergency alert system test and present my tablet to him.

"The zeros and ones that scrolled across the screen during the last emergency system test were binary code," I say. "This is the translation."

"Any idea what was going on in Conference Room Twelve last night?" Seven asks him.

"No," Ryan says.

"We checked that room on the map after the message was sent," I say. "There were thirty-two people in there, but the cameras were disabled. And when the room emptied, the cameras outside were disabled too. They came back online about thirty minutes later."

"What cameras?" Ryan asks.

I bring up the compound map that shows the locations of the cameras. "The red dots are security cameras." I hover my finger over one and video footage pops up.

"How did you find—?" he starts.

"Murphy figured it out," I say. "And we discovered something strange." I access the video feed of the mystery people in the enlisted recreation room, and I continue, "This rec room shows an occupancy of zero on the main map, but the video shows that there are people in there …"

Ryan zooms in on one of the faces and inhales. *He recognizes them!*

"Who are they?" I ask.

Ryan seems not to hear me. For the next several seconds, his fingers move quickly, zooming in and out on each person in the room, then he finally speaks, "They're the survivors of The Great Warrior Massacre."

"Why are they hiding them here?" Seven asks.

"I have no idea," Ryan says. "The commander told me they were dead."

THURSDAY, JUNE 30

1227

JACKIE

My secret communication system still shows no new messages. I need to accept the fact that I am alone now. The sole survivor of all of my people.

What happened to the five who survived the initial execution? Did they fall victim to an accident? Did the military find them and execute them? Or were they killed by another tribe of Outsiders? Even if they are still alive, out there on their own, four adults and one child have little chance of survival.

If my identity is discovered, the most likely scenario is that I'd be sent to Terminal Transfer, like Ray. Then I'd live the rest of my life in a solitary cell with no human contact. I've never been to the Terminal Transfer facility in person, but I've visited virtually. The visit was part of our boot camp experience. Prisoners at Terminal Transfer receive their food through a hatch in their cell. There is no sound other than your own voice. No touch other than your own touch. There is no stimulation other than your own mind. Most prisoners begin to display signs of mental illness after just a few weeks. Many attempt to take their own lives. During my virtual visit, I saw terrible bloody images that I will never be able to wipe from my memory.

With bleary eyes, I rummage through the classified documents that I accessed using Ten's instructions. I'm not actually sure what I'm looking for. There is nothing that I can find that can help my people anymore—

A folder name pops up that gets my attention: VAN_NUYS_RESOURCES.

Van Nuys? Nine months ago, when I assisted Murphy on her mission to sneak into her old compound, we landed at Van Nuys airport. Apparently, the compound where Murphy and Hanson and all of the other warriors grew up is located underground there. Very few people know about the compound's location. It requires an advanced security clearance to visit it. I don't have that clearance. I never would have known where the compound was if it wasn't for my involvement in Murphy's forbidden mission.

I start decryption on the VAN_NUYS_RESOURCES folder, and one by one the individual filenames appear on the screen:

TWO_THOUSAND_FIFTY-THREE

TWO_THOUSAND_FIFTY-TWO
TWO_THOUSAND_FIFTY-ONE
TWO_THOUSAND_FIFTY
TWO_THOUSAND_FORTY-NINE

And so on. The filenames are all numbers, in descending order. I decrypt the first one and open it. Inside is a photo of a baby, along with a date of birth. The child is just over two months old. The baby's file looks similar to our personnel files. It lists the child's parents, along with their photos. When I click on the woman, a new file opens. I decrypt it and find information about the child's mother. A young woman, nineteen years old. Her file is extremely long. Much longer than any of our personnel files. It starts with her birth.

Murphy and Hanson's files might be in this folder. I suppose I should learn as much information about these two as possible, especially considering how intimately the military considers me to be involved with them.

I click on the next file in the list: TWO_THOUSAND_FIFTY-TWO. Another infant. This one's a girl. Born two days before the other infant. I am about to go back to the main folder when something catches my eye. The images of the baby's parents. The woman … is Murphy. The man is Hanson.

But that's impossible. Murphy didn't give birth two

months ago. When this child was born, Murphy was being held as a prisoner at our compound.

I continue reading about the child. The infant's birth weight was seven pounds fourteen ounces. Her first medical evaluation was normal. Her next one is scheduled for July tenth, when she will be three months old. The baby feeds and sleeps well. She has begun to smile in response to human faces. There are videos too, of a baby girl whose eyes remind me of Murphy's and whose hair reminds me of Hanson's. At the end of one video, the baby smiles a broad, delighted smile, although I can't see what she's responding to. In another, a woman who isn't Murphy is holding the baby and the infant is crying inconsolably. I wish I could reach through the screen and hold her. I feel like I could comfort the baby better than that woman.

Is this infant *actually* Hanson and Murphy's child? It seems impossible based on the birth date, but maybe there is some explanation. Maybe babies are born differently there. In some sort of laboratory rather than from the woman's body. I wonder if Murphy and Hanson even know that they have a baby.

I continue reading, taking in the intricate details of the child's life. Until I reach the end of the file, where I find something that nearly stops my heart. The final entry:

ASSESSMENT:

PRODUCT OF UNAUTHORIZED BREEDING.

PLAN:
TERMINAL TRANSFER AT THREE MONTHS OF
AGE.

A date is listed: July tenth. The date of her next medical evaluation.

Less than two weeks from now.

I didn't know that they sent *babies* to Terminal Transfer, but why not, the military thought nothing of killing my people, whose only crime was that they were Outsiders. What would stop them from sentencing this baby to a life worse than death? Why would it matter to them that her only crime was being born?

THURSDAY, JUNE 30
1255

SEVEN

As I settle into my seat for our first class of the afternoon, my navigator vibrates. I check the screen and find a message from Jackie:

I'd like to speak with you in your quarters after dinner.
1900.

Ten and I have so much to do after dinner. Especially now that we learned that warriors who were supposed to be dead are secretly living here at the warrior compound, and that the commander lied about this fact to Ryan. But I reply to Jackie:

Yes. See you at 1900.

After dinner, Ten walks me to my quarters. It's only

1856, but Jackie is already waiting at my door. "I'll give you two some privacy," Ten says to us.

Jackie shakes her head. "Actually, what I have to say involves both of you."

I scan open the door to my quarters and the three of us go inside. Ten and I sit together on my bed and Jackie sits on the chair at my desk. She unfolds her tablet as she continues, "I was looking through the classified documents and discovered something concerning. It appears that the two of you have a baby …"

Ten straightens up. "Where did you see that?"

Jackie passes her tablet to us and I feel my breath leave me. On the screen is an image of Fifty-two—obtained today according to the date stamp. Below that are images of me … and Ten.

"Did you know about her?" Jackie asks us.

It doesn't make sense to deny it to Jackie. The truth is right there below the image of our beautiful baby girl. "How did they find out?" I breathe.

Jackie scrolls the screen down to the bottom. I read the words there and everything inside me stops. Ten's arms close around me and pull me protectively to him.

"They're going to send her to Terminal Transfer," I whisper in disbelief. "How could they do that? She's just a baby. I'm the one who should be transferred—"

"You should look at your files as well," Jackie says.

I feel Ten's hands manipulating the tablet. I wipe my tears away with my fist. Whatever is in our files, I need to see it. Ten opens mine first. My entire life is documented there, along with images and video, as if my story is some sort of illustrated fairytale presented for entertainment. There are videos of the baby who I once was but don't remember. And then I'm a toddler in the preschool classroom. My little hands reach out and touch little Ten's hands. The video ends just before we are pulled apart and scolded.

There's footage of Ten and me, behind the fish tank. A restricted area. One where I'd thought no one was watching. I scroll down the page, feeling more violated with each video I see. I scroll faster and faster, trying to get past it all, but I can't help seeing a video of Ten and me undressed in the laundry room. Touching each other's bodies. The thought that someone else saw these private personal moments makes acid rise up into my chest.

Some text catches my eye because, unlike all of the other entries, it is in red. I stop scrolling and read it: "EXCHANGED IDENTIFICATION MICROCHIP WITH TWO THOUSAND SIX. ASSISTED BY TWO THOUSAND TEN." There is video to illustrate this. Of Six and me in the drone closet with Ten. I scroll back. There are no previous such entries.

"They only saw the last switch," I say. "They must

have figured out the others."

"How many times did you switch places?" Jackie asks.

"Three," I say as I scroll through the rest of my file, feeling my life shatter inside me.

At the very bottom of the file is an assessment:

SUPERIOR CREATIVITY AND INTELLIGENCE.
UNACCEPTABLE DEFIANCE OF AUTHORITY.

And the plan:

REMEDIATION.
CONSIDER TERMINAL TRANSFER.

"I don't care if they transfer *me*," I say. "But Fifty-two … She's too little. If they transfer her, she'll …"

"We'll stop it," Ten says, folding me into his arms again. "I promise."

THURSDAY, JUNE 30
1906

TEN

At the same time as I say the words, I admit to myself
that I have no idea how to stop this. The military has been
watching us, even when we thought we were far beyond
their sights. They know some of our deepest secrets and
they haven't let on. They've been waiting to see what we
will do next. Ready to destroy us whenever they deem fit.

Jackie suggests that we pull up my file also and so I
do. It is not unlike Seven's. Private moments captured on
video from security cameras that I'd been told were
unwatched. I should never have trusted that they'd been
abandoned. How could I have trusted anything in a place so
filled with lies?

There is also footage from cameras I never knew were
there. I never saw cameras in the room behind the fish tank,
or in the restricted hallways, or in the laundry room, but
there were cameras there watching us. At least there are no

images from the drone tunnel where Seven and I used to hide from sight. Or from our domiciles, both back home and here at the warrior compound. At least there were some places where we were unrecorded. At least Seven and I were alone with each other when we lost control.

I'm prepared for the worst by the time I get to the end of my file. The assessment:

SUPERIOR CREATIVITY AND INTELLIGENCE.
WILLINGNESS TO DEFY AUTHORITY.

And the plan:

CLOSE OBSERVATION.
CONSIDER TERMINAL TRANSFER.

It is strange that they don't consider my crimes as egregious as Seven's. I suppose the fact that I mated with her is probably accepted by the military, given that they seem to be taking no steps to prevent any of the warriors from spending private time alone in each other's quarters.

The only infraction they've noted in red is assisting Seven and her sister with their microchip switch. Even the touching we did as children seems to have been overlooked, which is strange considering that it was a direct violation of the Rules of Life.

And so it appears that *I* am not in imminent danger, but Seven and our baby are. If we do nothing, Fifty-two will be sent off to Terminal Transfer in a matter of days. The thought of that makes something inside me crack open, releasing cold liquid anger. As long as I am living, I won't allow harm to come to Seven or Fifty-two. If they are harmed, I will die a thousand times over. And so, I will fight for them, even if the consequence is my own demise. I will do whatever it takes to save them. But I know that even my best efforts could fail.

THURSDAY, JUNE 30
1957

SEVEN

After Jackie leaves, Ten and I hold each other. We give ourselves exactly five minutes to grieve for the loss of the future life for our child and ourselves that we'd thought we'd ensured. Then we send a message to Ryan, asking him to meet us in the little white room.

He greets us at the door, his expression troubled even though we have not yet shared our news with him. After he scans us into the room, he deposits himself in a chair with an uneasy sigh. "What did you find?"

"We got access to our personal files," Ten says. "And the file for our baby." Rather than explain further, he passes his tablet to Ryan. On it is Fifty-two's file.

Ryan reads the information there, his brow creased with concern. I can tell when he gets to the assessment and plan for her because he takes a deep breath and closes his eyes. His hand goes to his forehead and he presses hard on his temples. "Okay," he says.

"Okay?" I repeat. "They're going to send our baby to prison!"

"I'll figure something out," he says weakly.

"We don't have time for that! We need to do something now!" I'm not upset with Ryan. I just can't hold in my pain anymore. Everything in my life is ripping apart. "This can't wait until—"

"Seven!" Ryan grabs both my arms, stopping me not by his actions, but by the fact that he just called me by my real name. My forbidden name.

I look into his eyes. They're tired. "I can't let them hurt her," I say desperately.

"I understand," he says.

"I need a plan," I insist.

"I need a lot of plans, Murphy," he says. "There are many people in danger right now."

"Who else is in danger?" I ask.

"The Great Warrior Massacre survivors," Ryan says quietly. "The military has been gathering information from them, questioning them about the Outsiders. Once that's completed, they're planning to send them to Terminal Transfer. The military considers them far too dangerous to keep anywhere else. The survivors probably have no idea that they're in grave danger." He inhales. "I grew up with those people. They were my friends. A few months ago, they risked their lives to save my life and your sister's. I owe them everything."

"Can you stop them from being transferred?" Ten asks.

"Not through traditional channels," Ryan says. "In order to prevent their transfer, I'm going to have to shake up this entire place …"

"We'll help," Ten says.

"Yes," I agree.

"Absolutely not. I will not involve you in any of that," Ryan says. "Go back to your quarters and start thinking about a plan to help your baby. We'll meet again tomorrow and—"

"What if we could do both?" I ask.

Ryan puts his hand on my shoulder and takes hold firmly. "We *will* do both."

"I mean at the same time," I say. "If we're going to help Fifty-two, we'll have to change the way things operate back home. And if we're going to rescue the Great Warrior Massacre survivors, things are going to have to change here. But the two compounds are connected, aren't they? The people in charge here are the same ones who are in charge back home. Those are the people who we need to stop and we only need to stop them once."

"It isn't so simple," Ryan says. "The people in charge aren't easy to stop."

"We have to disable them," Ten says.

"And how do you propose we do that?" Ryan asks.

Ten inhales uncertainly. "I'm not sure if it will work, but I have an idea."

SUNDAY, JULY 3
2114

TEN

Over the next several days, Ryan, Seven, Jackie, and I build a plan—with the help of other people who Ryan said we can trust—to escape from the warrior compound and go back home to tell people the truth. On the final night before our mission, I'm not sure whether it's exhaustion or accomplishment that leads Ryan to finally insist that we go get some sleep. Likely it's both. We've built a solid framework, and we've extensively considered our contingency plans for worst-case scenarios. Still, there are so many ways that our plan could go wrong.

We don't bother with goodnights. Ryan scans us out of the little white room, and Seven and I go back to her quarters and undress for bed. Then she stands before me, naked, and I look at her, as if for the first time. Shadows fall over her, dappling her skin in light and dark. She is stunning.

I feel the intense urge, the need, to mate with her. I press my lips to hers and take her into my arms. Instantly, I feel her tension drain away, replaced with urgent energy. We lower ourselves onto the bed, and her body accepts mine. Seven's warmth takes over my thoughts. My awareness ends at her and me. Our movements are aggressive and fierce. But then we still ourselves. Seven is trembling, as if she's afraid to let go. I lightly run my hand along the side of her face and into her hair. She shivers and winces, as if she is in pain, but the soft sound that escapes her lips tells me her experience is far from painful. I take a deep, shaky breath and it happens. Her energy envelops me and I release my energy into her.

And then we lie together. Quiet except for our quick breaths.

"Tomorrow, everything's going to change," Seven finally whispers with a mixture of anticipation and apprehension. "For us, and everyone we've ever known."

She's right. Whether or not our plan is successful, once it begins, everything will change irreversibly. We will never be able to go back to the way things were.

"Tomorrow could be the most important day in all of our lives," I agree.

I just hope it isn't the last.

MONDAY, JULY 4

0743

SEVEN

Today is the day we have chosen to act. So much needs to be accomplished all in one day for our plan to work. We have made few advanced preparations because we can't risk arousing suspicion at a time when the military seems to be on high alert.

We start the morning proceeding with our routine schedules. I go to rehab for my last day ever at Carter's mercy.

After the purple pod finishes its torture of me, Carter remarks that I seem more relaxed today. But I'm not relaxed. I am focused. On doing what I need to do to save my baby. I feel like I see everything more clearly than usual, like wherever I put my focus is magnified so that I can see the slightest detail without any distractions.

The pod deposits me on the treadmill and Carter straps

the shock belt around my waist. The treadmill starts to move. My joints and muscles ache in protest as I walk in step with it. I'm half-expecting Carter to shock me, just to try to get a reaction out of me, when a high-pitched beep from my navigator startles me into tripping on my own feet. The shock belt catches me, but it doesn't deliver a shock. The treadmill waits for me to regain my footing, before it continues at a slightly slower pace.

A quick look at my navigator confirms that the beep indicates yet another test of the emergency alert system. These tests have been coming nearly every day. We discovered that the number of phrases encoded in the zeros and ones matches the number of people who occupy the designated conference room a few minutes later. The phrases must be codenames for the people attending the meeting. By monitoring the security cameras in nearby hallways, we've seen that certain individuals—mostly senior officers—consistently appear to be leaving the area of the meetings. Twice, we saw Carter among them.

I glance over at her, expecting her to scold me for my clumsiness on the treadmill, or at least give me some instructions, but she is focused on her navigator. Looking at the zeros and ones. Unblinking. As if she can read them. I swallow and focus on my walking until she says, "That will be all for today. Go ahead and get dressed."

It isn't time for our session to end yet. It's only 0746.

In the past, Carter has ended every session promptly at the scheduled finish time: 0800. She's not ending the session early for my benefit. I have no doubt about that. She has received an order to attend an emergency meeting.

Carter removes my monitor wires and I finally allow myself to look at her and consider the thoughts screaming in my head. Her eyes are somewhat bloodshot. The skin underneath them is slightly dark, as if she hasn't had a good night's sleep in a while. Her face is flawed, like mine, like all people. But when I look into her eyes now I notice something that sends a cold shiver over my skin. It's something barely perceptible. Something I can't quite put into words. Something I've seen—a very few times—in the eyes of Miss Teresa and Professor Adam.

Robots rarely allow people to lock gazes with them. They almost always seem to find an elegant reason to look away. Their behavior reads as socially-acceptable shyness. But on those rare occasions that I've looked into their eyes, I've seen proof that they weren't like us. An ever-so-subtle vacancy. An emptiness.

Carter isn't cautious about me looking into her eyes. She is perfectly imperfect, like all humans. But she is vicious in a way that I thought humans couldn't be. Even more cruel than Twelve. She seems to lacking in compassion and empathy. I've never seen anyone act in this way. Her behavior doesn't seem human.

I look away from her quickly, so she doesn't sense the thoughts running through my head.

Maybe Carter *isn't* human.

MONDAY, JULY 4

0803

TEN

"I need to talk to you," Seven says, her tone grave.

My body tenses. We can't afford for anything to go wrong right now. It's too late to make any major changes to the plan for today's mission. If we discover significant issues, we might have to postpone. And Ryan's intel is that the Great Warrior Massacre survivors will be sent to Terminal Transfer tonight. If we aren't able to successfully carry out our mission today, we will lose them.

I follow her from our underwater classroom to her quarters. We only have a few minutes before class and so we shouldn't be going off on our own, but even without her telling me, I know that what Seven has to say must be said, and it must be done in private.

She scans her door closed behind us and then turns to me. "I think Carter might be a robot," she whispers.

That doesn't make any sense. If Carter is a robot, it

shouldn't have taken Seven this long to realize it. Robots do look very much like humans, but there are subtle signs that are easy to detect if you look closely.

Seven's words continue to spill out, fast, "She isn't like the robots back home or the ones we've seen here. She's nearly indistinguishable from a human being. I never would have considered it if we hadn't had that emergency alert. I saw her looking at the zeros and ones as if she were reading them. Then she ended our session early."

"That doesn't prove she's a robot," I counter. "She was probably just noting that there was code there that needed to be deciphered. Maybe she recorded the code and decoded it after you left."

"After the code ran, I looked into her eyes," Seven says. "There was something missing. That spark of life that we all have. She didn't have that."

I know the spark that she's referring to. "Are you sure?"

"I'm positive," she says, and then she inhales and her expression grows even more troubled. "What if the commander is a robot too? He's the one who must be sending out the code, right?"

"The commander isn't a robot," I say. "We've seen him eat and drink. And sweat. Robots don't sweat."

"Maybe here they do."

Cold discomfort burrows into my skin. Is this

possible? Could there be robots so indistinguishable from us that they blend in completely? So much like us that we could fail to detect that they are not human? Whether or not we can confirm Seven's theory, we should at least consider it.

And then I realize something that sends a hard lump into my throat. The first part of our plan involves Seven interacting with the commander. "If the commander is a robot, it could affect the way he reacts to you," I say. "If he isn't human, this might not work."

"It's too late to change our plan," she says. "I think we should proceed."

When I look into her eyes, I know there is nothing I can say to change her mind.

MONDAY, JULY 4

1218

SEVEN

The commander eats his lunch in the officers' main dining room every day from 1200 to 1220, like clockwork, and so I wait outside, ready to ambush him. It is the first step in our mission.

As the time on my navigator clicks from 1219 to 1220, the door to the officers' dining room slides open and the commander strides into the hallway.

"Commander, may I speak with you, sir?" I ask him.

He barely glances in my direction. "I'm quite busy, Murphy."

I didn't think my pulse could race any faster, but it does. If the commander refuses my request, it will be the first failure in our mission. We will move into our contingency plan for this scenario which isn't nearly as good.

"Please, sir, this is very important to me," I try, the

desperation breaking into my voice.

He gives a small sigh and stops. "Okay, go ahead."

I swallow. "I need to speak with you in private."

It might be only because he has already agreed to speak with me that the commander leads me down the dark hall that goes to his office. My hand trembles as I fall into step behind him and activate my navigator. The commander scans open the first door and I let my left wrist brush the spot where the scanner seems to be hidden. I try to make my movement appear natural. I know that there are cameras watching me. I can't do anything to arouse suspicion.

I furtively sneak a look at the navigator's screen. *Nothing.*

The second door slides open. I get my left wrist closer to the wall this time.

Nothing.

Maybe I should have let Ten do this. But I insisted. Because I am the one who put Ten at risk. If I hadn't switched places with my sister, he would never have been in this position.

Or maybe he would have. If Ten had come here without me, I wonder if he would have decided on his own to change things …

The third door opens.

I practically slam my navigator against the wall, targeting the exact spot where the commander scanned his arm.

I look at my navigator's screen.

Success. I have the commander's precious access code. A code so protected that it changes daily. I've accomplished my first goal for the mission. Now I just need to buy some time until Ten can accomplish his task.

The fourth door opens. Then the fifth. And then a silver door that opens into the commander's office. He sits behind his desk and gestures for me to take a seat opposite him. I look at his eyes, trying to see if I perceive that same vacancy that I saw in Carter's. But he's too far away from me. From this distance, I don't think I'd be able to see it.

"Yes?" the commander says. I was probably staring at him far too long to be socially acceptable.

"My question is kind of personal, sir," I say, squeezing my perspiring hands together in my lap.

"Thus the need to speak privately," he says, appearing impatient. "Get on with it, Murphy."

"Will I ever be allowed to have children, sir?" I blurt out.

The commander exhales. Frustrated, maybe. "May I offer you some advice?"

I nod. "Of course, sir."

"If you ask enough questions about your life, the answers will eventually disappoint you."

That just might be the most disconcerting thing ever

said to me and, even more disturbingly, it feels familiar. I've heard that exact statement before. When I was very young. I'd forgotten it until this moment, possibly intentionally. "That sounds like something my mother once said to me," I whisper.

The commander seems pleased by my statement. A smile begins to form on his lips. But as he opens his mouth to respond, both of our navigators emit a shrill beep that I recognize instantly. The emergency alert system test. Only this one is not like the others.

This message was sent by Ten.

The commander's gaze jumps to his navigator, but almost immediately it is back on me. He stands. I stand too. It's clear that our meeting is over.

"I must get on with my schedule," he says coolly.

He should be flustered. He just received a message that he was not expecting. If our theory regarding the clandestine meetings is correct, the commander is responsible for the coded emergency alert messages, and so this one should disturb him—whether or not he has decoded the contents—because he did not authorize it to be sent. But the commander is undeniably calm. His breaths are steady. His face doesn't show even the slightest hint of distress.

"I trust I've answered your question," he says as he approaches the door. His body is now inches away from mine.

I force myself not to consider the thought that is overtaking my mind as I look into his dark-brown eyes. The vacancy there is so clear that I can't believe I never noticed it before. "Yes, sir," I say. "You have."

Without warning, he pulls me tight against him, his arm unyielding around my neck. Panic pulses into my arteries. I feel the instinctive urge to fight, but I suppress it. It makes no sense to fight the commander. I mustn't anger him. He could kill me quickly here, with no witnesses.

"What are you doing, sir?" I ask, trying to keep my voice steady.

"I'm going to have to ask you to wait here," he says, so calmly that it makes my skin ice cold. "Please have a seat until I return." He pushes me back into the chair that I occupied moments ago and scans his wrist near the armrest. In an instant, I am tethered to the seat by straps across my arms, legs, and chest.

"Why must I wait here, sir?" I ask, truly uncertain of my exact crime.

"I'm sensing that you're a bit confused about something and I'm going to need to clarify it for you. But there's an urgent matter that I need to attend to right now. I will return shortly. Please wait calmly until I do."

I want to cry. I want to scream. But I hold in my emotions. My only hope is to obey his order. "Yes, sir," I force out, but my words are interrupted by a dreadful thought.

The commander would never restrain me like this if he was ever planning to let me go.

MONDAY, JULY 4

1226

TEN

There are no security cameras in the commander's office, at least none that I know of, and so I watch the video feed from the closest camera to his office that I have access to. A camera that faces the first of the six doors that secure the commander's office and private hallway.

Seven has been inside the office for several minutes. Two minutes have passed since I sent the coded message regarding an urgent meeting in Conference Room 24. I listed the codenames of everyone who has attended any of the commanders' secret meetings in the past few days. We expected that the commander would respond swiftly to his receipt of my message. He would be quick to investigate who called the meeting and why.

As each second passes, concern builds in my core. Something isn't right. The commander should have responded by now. Something is delaying him. But what?

Suddenly, I see what I've been waiting for. The security video shows the first door slide open and the commander passes through the open doorway. I feel a bit of relief, until I notice the empty space all around him. Seven isn't with him.

Where is Seven?

As far as I know, there are no other exits from the commander's office. If Seven isn't with the commander, she must still be inside the office. But he would surely never leave her there alone. Even if he had absolutely nothing to hide, he wouldn't allow her to stay unguarded in his personal space. Unless she no longer posed a threat … unless she's …

I jump to my feet. I have to fight to keep myself from running as I travel the short stretch of hallway from the command center to the commander's office. What I am about to do will jeopardize our entire mission, but without my actions we will be unable to complete it. And besides, the only thing I care about right now is finding Seven.

I ready my navigator to capture a code and I pull off my warrior necklace, gripping it tightly in my hand. I approach the first door, knowing that in just a moment I will blow our cover. I will be seen on camera accessing an area that I should not have access to. If anyone is watching—which someone surely must be—the pursuit will begin.

As rapidly as I can, I grab an access code from the first door's scanner and transfer it to the chip in my warrior necklace. I scan the necklace and the door slides open. I access the next door and the next. All the way to the silver door. I don't allow myself to consider what I will find on the other side. I scan the door open, ready to grab Seven in whatever state she's in and run.

But I can't.

"Ten!" she says so quietly that it scares me. Seven is tied to a chair. Tears fill her eyes. She looks more frightened than I've ever seen her.

"I'm going to get you out of here," I say with a confidence I don't feel.

"The right armrest," she says. "There's some kind of scanner that controls the restraints."

I search for the scanner but see nothing, and so I attempt to scan my warrior necklace blindly in response to Seven's suggestions, "I think it's higher and to the right. Maybe a little higher." I must hit the correct spot, because the straps suddenly release. Seven jumps up. "We need to get out of here."

I scan open the doors in our path as my heart pounds at least a hundred times per minute. The opening of each door could reveal someone sent to stop us, but when we make it through the final door, no one is waiting.

"This way," I breathe, heading off to the right. To the

command center.

I open the door and scan the commander's code at the panel that activates the monitors. As I race to the monitor Ryan told me about, I activate my tablet and hand it to Seven.

"Watch the security footage," I tell her. "Let me know if anyone is coming."

"Got it," she says, and I turn my focus to the task at hand.

There is a lockdown feature accessible only in the command center. Only the commander or a combination of three senior officers is able to access it. With the commander's code, I open up the system. From here, I can lock any door. When a door is locked-down, a sheet of impenetrable material is passed through it, making it impossible to pass until the lockdown is lifted. The lock is permanent until it is relieved here at the command center. No one can open a locked-down door at the door itself, not even the commander.

"There are three soldiers coming this way fast!" Seven reports.

I look over at my tablet and see the soldiers hurriedly heading down a nearby hallway. I don't know for certain that we are their targets, but we can't take any chances. I reach up to the screen on the wall in front of me and swipe my warrior necklace over the door that the soldiers are approaching. It's an emergency door only. It's normally kept open, just like it is right now. In the graphic on the screen, I watch it close in response to my actions. A message pops up above the screen:

Scan access code to confirm lockdown.

I hold the warrior charm up to the screen.
The image of the door turns red.

Lockdown confirmed.

I lock the door behind the soldiers too, trapping them in the hallway. Just to be cautious, I lock all of the other doors leading to the command center as well.

"We're safe," I say to Seven. "At least for the moment. Where's the commander?"

Seven switches to a view from one of the cameras inside Conference Room 24. The room is filled with people—likely everyone who I invited there via my message.

But there is one person who I'd hoped wouldn't make it: the commander.

We chose the furthest conference room from the commander's office, hoping that all of the others who were invited to the meeting would arrive before the commander did. The plan was to trap the commander in a hallway, sandwiched between two locked doors. Isolating him from those inside the conference room. Preventing him from giving them any instructions.

Now we have no choice but to lock the commander inside the conference room with the others. I swipe my warrior necklace over the conference room door, and the lockdown message pops up. I hold my warrior charm to the screen, and the image of the door to the conference room turns red.

Lockdown confirmed.

"It isn't the way we planned," I say to Seven, "but it's done."

MONDAY, JULY 4
1236

JACKIE

I think I just heard the conference room door lock
down. The locking of the conference room door is long
overdue. Something must have delayed Ten.

The commander entered the conference room a full
minute ago. In our plan, he was never supposed to enter it
at all. The door is soundproof and so I have no idea what is
happening inside the room, but I'm sure that, once the
commander realizes that something beyond his reach is
happening, he will send teams throughout the compound to
investigate. Ten has already hijacked the outgoing
communications for the navigators of all of the attendees of
this bogus meeting, but nothing is preventing the people in
the room from physically going out to investigate. Nothing
except a locked-down door.

I quietly approach the conference room door and scan
the chip that has been implanted in my arm ever since I

arrived here.

Access denied. Lockdown in effect.

I exhale fully for the first time in hours and send Ten a message:

We're good.

MONDAY, JULY 4
1237

SEVEN

We've completed the first stage in our plan. The
commander and his conspirators are now secured in the
conference room. There is no way for them to get out until
we release them.

Ten pulls me into his arms and holds me tightly.
"What happened in the commander's office?" he asks.

"He said that I seemed confused about something and
he needed to clarify it for me," I say. "Then he strapped me
to the chair. I'm sure he was planning to come back and
question me, and then eliminate me."

"Are you okay?" he asks, looking into my eyes.

"Yes, I'm fine," I say, even though I'm not. I must
remain strong right now. "We need to send out the next
message."

Ten composes another emergency alert system
message, but this one is much different from the last. It

says, in capital letters across the top of the screen:

THIS IS NOT A TEST.

His message orders all personnel to evacuate immediately to the beach. No one is to stay behind. When they arrive on the beach, Jackie and some of our trusted warriors and soldiers will tell everyone the truth about what is going on here. That the people in charge are manipulating us. Lying to us. Each lie will be exposed, along with the evidence we've found to support the truth. Hopefully, people will trust what they hear. We will need all the support we can get in the days, weeks, and months that follow.

Ten sends the message and then checks the compound security cameras. Everyone appears to be evacuating, except for the soldiers that Ten trapped in the hallway of course.

"All right," Ten says, pointing at the locked-down door that is preventing the soldiers' escape. "I'm going to open that door."

I nod, and Ten scans open the door that traps the soldiers, keeping their path to us blocked. The soldiers head toward the airlock.

I exhale with relief. "They're evacuating the compound."

"Good," he says. "Let's get to the drone hangar."

Before we leave the command center, Ten shuts down all of the monitors, leaving the hollow room lit only by soft blue utility lights. He scans open the door and I force my eyes to adjust to the brightness of the hallway. We walk briskly toward the hangar, but not too fast, hoping to avoid arousing suspicion.

The hallways are filled with people who are obediently evacuating the compound. We move through the teeming corridors, sometimes traveling with the pressured flow, sometimes against it. I keep an eye on everyone who gets close to us, remaining ready to fight any hand that might reach out to grab us but, by the time we arrive at the drone hangar, none has.

I wonder where Ryan is now. He was supposed to break into the enlisted quarters where the Great Warrior Massacre survivors were being held and help them to escape, but any number of problems could have befallen him. Ryan told us that we should carry on with the next step in our mission regardless of whether his part of the plan was successful. He said that we were not even to check the security cameras to see how he was doing until we were strapped into our seats on the drone.

Ten and I climb the short ramp that leads into our assigned drone. Ten enters first and so he sees what's inside before I do. "Ryan!" he practically shouts.

I follow Ten into the drone and see Ryan sitting in a seat, being tended to by a woman who wears a white jumpsuit; she must be one of the nine survivors of the Great Warrior Massacre. A significant amount of bright red blood trickles down the side of Ryan's face, but he appears alert.

"Are you okay?" I ask as I rush to him. I gesture for the woman to lift the gauze that she has pressed on the side of his head, so I can check his wound.

"Let her look," Ryan says to the woman. "Murphy has some medical training."

She lifts the gauze and I nearly lose my breath. Ryan's cuts are deep. Very deep. And bleeding heavily. Some of the small arteries of his scalp may have been severed. His wounds need to be treated before he loses too much blood.

"Prepare for takeoff," someone commands as the door is sealed shut.

"Can you fix me up while we travel?" Ryan asks.

The traveling isn't really the problem. "I've never treated a wound this significant," I admit. I've only seen a few lacerations and none were this severe.

But Ryan wasn't talking to me. He was talking to the woman in the white jumpsuit.

"Not a problem," she says to him. "I've seen plenty worse." She hands me the first aid kit. "I could use some help though."

As the platform beneath the drone rises up to the level

of the open ceiling, the woman lays out some medical supplies on a sterile drape. She hands me a pair of gloves and then some gauze. "See if you can blot up a bit of the blood," she says. "I need to find the bleeder."

I use the gauze to staunch the remarkable amount of blood that's rushing from the wound. The woman's hands work as deftly as a robot surgeon's. Somehow in the mess, she finds a tiny artery that squirts blood with every beat of Ryan's heart. It looks much too little to account for all the bleeding, but when she zaps it with a coagulator and I dab the area, the bleeding has slowed to a gentle ooze.

"Are you a doctor?" I ask the woman.

Her eyes remain focused on her work. "I do the best I can."

"When she was living with the Outsiders, Maria saw more illnesses and injuries than a doctor back home would see in a thousand lifetimes," Ryan says.

"And you were a warrior once?" Ten asks her.

"Ryan and I grew up together …" Her voice trails off. At first I think it's because she is concentrating on her work, but then I wonder if maybe it's something more.

"Were the two of you friends?" I ask.

"Maria was my closest friend," Ryan says. "When she was chosen to be a warrior, I was devastated. Up until a few months ago, I thought she was dead …"

Maria's gaze meets Ryan's for just a moment and I see

a connection. The kind of connection I saw between him and Ma'am. *Ryan once loved Maria.* I think he still does.

As Maria begins to seal Ryan's wound, I consider the next stage in our plan. It could prove to be the most difficult. When we arrive at our home compound, we will need to tell everyone the truth about Up Here. We must convince them to believe us. We will only get one chance.

And if we fail, the consequences could be deadly.

MONDAY, JULY 4
1246

JACKIE

Everyone has been accounted for. Those who are not locked in Conference Room 24 or in a drone traveling to Murphy's old compound are now assembled on the beach, the same way they have been at every muster drill I've experienced since I came here. Orderly and controlled. Exactly how those in charge would like things to be.

But what is about to happen will change that order permanently. Soon there will be new leaders. Ryan has suggested that at least one of our leaders should be chosen from the nine Great Warrior Massacre survivors who were removed from the Outsider compound before it was destroyed. I hope that comes to pass. Those people have special insight into the plight of those outside the government's control. I think they would be ideal leaders. They would work for the good of all rather than just a select few.

The changes that will follow will come too late for my people, but at least they will come. The deaths of my fellow Outsiders will be avenged with good. That is what most of them would have wanted. And when I really think about it, despite all the anger inside me, all the pain and the loss and the hurt, that is what I want too. When I leave this planet, I want it to be a better place than it was when I arrived on it. If this mission succeeds, it will be.

I give the signal, and a few members of the crowd step forward. Some are warriors. The rest are soldiers of various ranks, from officer to enlisted. There are no senior officers among them. Every one of the senior officers is locked inside the conference room, probably wondering what the hell is going on out here.

The speakers gather, facing the crowd. Microphone drones hover at their lips. The first to speak is Warrior Representative Edwards.

"We have some important information to share with you this afternoon," she begins. "This information may be difficult to accept, but I promise you that what we are about to say is, to the best of our knowledge, the complete and honest truth. You have been misled by those who you trusted to lead you. We all have. But that is about to change …"

Slowly, she begins to share what we have learned. Classified documents are projected into the air. Video is presented. I look out at those listening to the overwhelming evidence of the lies we've been told. Some of the faces show doubt, even resistance, but I also see expressions of understanding and compassion. When Edwards reveals the facts about the murder of my tribe of Outsiders, illustrated by graphic footage that I can't bear to watch, tears are shed, not only by me, but by some my fellow soldiers.

Many challenges lie ahead of us. But I am beginning to believe they will not be faced unaided. There are people here will fight alongside us.

A sense of calm comes over me. A sense of belonging to something much bigger than myself. A feeling I haven't had since—

BOOM.

An explosive blast throws me forward, planting my face inches deep in the sand. Shards of jagged glass and metal rain down on me like hail, as a horrible thought sinks into me …

Whatever just happened wasn't part of our plan.

MONDAY, JULY 4
1314

TEN

Our aerial drone slams violently to the left, as if it was punched into a wall by a giant fist. Black chunks splash across the window, some of them leaving dark scratches in their wake. As the drone falls from the sky, I am hit with a horrible sense of déjà vu. For a moment, I am right back in a drone with Six and Ryan and Jackie, thinking that my life is about to end.

I shake away the memory and bring myself back into the present. Here with Seven. Instinctively, I've grabbed hold of her, which is good because, since she wasn't harnessed in, the turbulence would have knocked her off her feet. In my hands, she has regained her footing, even though the drone wavers, seeming uncertain as to whether it should rise or continue to fall.

Seven and I lock eyes, and I see her fear. I feel my own. Time seems to have slowed and sound has ceased to exist. My stomach feels alternately light and heavy. Have we been attacked? If so, there will surely be a second wave. I wonder if this might be the end of us.

But the drone shakily gains altitude. And no further attacks come.

"What the hell happened?" someone asks.

A soldier on the opposite side of the drone answers but, based on the dazed expression on her face, I'm not sure that she's speaking in response to his question. "The compound is gone."

I look at the ocean below us and feel the acid in my stomach rise up into my throat. Where the warrior compound once stood, there are now just splinters of glass and metal. Small fires burn here and there.

The compound is gone, along with all who remained inside it. Everyone who we trapped inside Conference Room 24 must now be dead. The only consolation I can find is that those mustered on the beach appear to have been out of range of the worst of it. Many more lives could have been lost today.

"How did the whole compound explode like that … all at once?" I ask in disbelief.

"There must have been a self-destruct mechanism," Ryan says. "Some modern military bases are built that way. To avoid having them fall into the wrong hands."

"But who activated it?" Seven asks, her eyes upset.

"Did one of *us* do this?"

"No," Ryan says. "It had to be the commander. I don't think anyone else has the authority."

"But how?" I ask. "He was locked in that conference room. How could he—?"

"It doesn't make any sense," Ryan says, appearing as distressed as I feel.

"Is there a self-destruct mechanism in the compound back home?" Seven whispers.

Ryan inhales. "I don't know."

MONDAY, JULY 4
1326

SEVEN

It is possible that everyone who once controlled us is now dead. But it is also possible that there are those in charge who we haven't yet identified. My daughter and the people back home might still be at risk. And so our mission must continue.

Now there is a new threat. One that we didn't consider during our mission preparation. One that we didn't plan for. If the warrior compound had a self-destruct mechanism, then it's possible that there's one back home as well. And if anyone with the authority to use it is not dead, or if those who are dead have already set a cascade in motion, every life back home is in imminent danger. And so our mission has changed. We will now need to perform, not just an education, but an evacuation.

Maria and I quickly finish with Ryan's wound, then she cleans the blood from his face and neck. Looking at him now, I'd never know he was injured. Ryan discusses our revised mission plan with everyone onboard and a cryptic message is sent to those in the drones accompanying us. Ryan thinks it could be dangerous to share anything important via the communication system. He'll quickly brief the people in the other drones when we land.

In the quiet that follows our discussion, I turn to Maria. "It must have been difficult being imprisoned by the Outsiders for so long."

"At the beginning we were prisoners," she says, looking down into her lap. "But we chose to stay."

"Why would you want to stay?" Ten asks.

"The military didn't want us back. They refused to negotiate for our release. The Outsiders planned to execute us, but we convinced them that we were more valuable alive than dead. They grudgingly decided to let us live. Very gradually, we proved our worth to them. After a few years passed, we were free to stay and go as we pleased." She looks up, finally making eye contact. "Our entire lives we'd been prisoners, just like you. At our birth compound. And at the military base. But with the Outsiders, we were finally free."

I get the feeling Maria doesn't know that her tribe has been destroyed. I suppose now isn't the time to tell her. She can be told tomorrow, when she will be able to properly grieve for the loss of the people she knew and the place she once called home. I wonder who will be tasked with telling her what she's lost. I guess it depends on who survives today.

"ETA five minutes," the pilot calls out, instantly bringing my thoughts back to our mission.

Ryan turns to Ten. "Send the message now."

Using the commander's hijacked account, Ten sends a message to the officer in charge of protecting our former compound. He tells her that there is a classified danger to those below ground. He states that troops will be arriving to evacuate the inhabitants and that a temporary evacuation center should be set up at least 500 yards away. A soldier who specializes in explosives recommended that distance in case there is a self-destruct mechanism in the compound. I only hope that if there is such a mechanism, it hasn't been activated already. That our compound hasn't yet been blown away.

I am relieved to see a quick response to Ten's message:

We will initiate evacuation protocol immediately.

I assume that means our compound is still intact.

Ten turns the screen of his navigator toward Ryan. "It sounds like they're cooperating."

"What's going to happen to the people who we

evacuate?" I ask.

"There's an old military base located in Santa Monica," Ryan says. "It's stocked with emergency supplies only, but we should be able to shuffle over some provisions from nearby compounds."

"Is the Santa Monica base safe?" I ask.

"It's as safe as anyplace right now," he says. "And it's much safer than the alternative."

I nod. I once thought The Box was the safest place there was. Right now, it could be the most dangerous.

"Where is the Terminal Transfer compound located?" Ten asks.

"That doesn't matter now," Ryan says.

"Of course it does," I argue. If today's operation goes horribly wrong, our daughter could still end up at the Terminal Transfer compound. And if Ryan dies today, Ten and I need to know where to find our baby. "If they end up sending Fifty-two there, we'll need to—"

"It's death," Ryan says, his voice low. "They take the person into an unmonitored room and give them an injection to kill them. I'm sorry I didn't tell you sooner. I didn't want to make this any worse for you than it already was."

They are planning to execute my daughter.

Ryan thought knowing that information would make this mission harder for me. In fact, it makes it easier.

237

Because now I am willing to do whatever I need to do to ensure its success. The consequences of failure are too great for anything less. This mission isn't just about making our existence better.

It is a matter of life and death.

MONDAY, JULY 4

1335

SIX

Lunchtime was extraordinarily pleasant today. I sat
with Nine, Three, and Four, and enjoyed a relaxed
conversation. The four of us are starting to become good
friends, at ease with one another. I envision our children
growing up together. Sharing meals. Conversations. I think
it will be—

Suddenly, a horrible sound rips through the air, like
my morning wake-up alarm but much louder, higher
pitched, and more insistent. The alarm finally quiets,
replaced by a calm female voice, "Ladies and gentlemen.
We will now proceed with an organized relocation. This is
a simple process designed to keep you safe and
comfortable. Please proceed immediately to the location
indicated now on the screen of your navigator. We will
refer to this location as your 'muster station.' Please
proceed there directly now. Do not return to your domiciles.

Do not collect your children from Infant Stim or School. They will reunite with you at your muster station."

I look to the screen of my navigator and see the words: Muster Station E Tenth Floor. Nine's navigator has the same information on it.

"What's an organized relocation?" Four asks.

"It sounds like we're going to go someplace," Nine says.

Three looks concerned. "Like Up There?"

I have a feeling that we are going above the sky. I can't imagine where else they could send us that would require this type of event.

"I need to pick up Fifty-two at Infant Stim," I whisper to my friends.

"But they said—" Four starts.

I shake my head. "I don't trust them," I murmur under my breath. It's a prohibited thing to say, but this situation demands it.

"I'll come with you," Nine says.

"Me too," Three says. "I need to get Fifty-one."

Four nods in agreement.

We all head to the door. My shoes and navigator direct me to turn right, but we go left. I assume there are multiple muster stations, because people are traveling in all different directions. Everyone seems remarkably composed, but I suppose that makes sense. The way the announcement presented what is happening, it sounded as if we have nothing to fear.

I disable the connection between my navigator and my shoes to stop the distracting vibrations around my feet, but the navigator furiously insists—via the flashing red text on its screen—that I reverse direction and proceed to my assigned station. After a few turns though, it finally accepts my route. I guess my muster station must be in this direction.

Two clunky, cabinet-like security drones roll slowly through the crowd. The red lights along their upper borders illuminate the surrounding walls in a spinning pattern. "Please proceed to your assigned muster stations in an orderly fashion," the drones broadcast in unison from their front speakers. "Step-by-step directions are provided to you via your navigator."

People obligingly make way for the drones, the way we have always been taught to do. But when I step aside to allow them to pass, the drones block Three's path and Four's as well.

"Two Thousand Three and Two Thousand Four, you are traveling in an unauthorized route," they say. "Please turn back and proceed to your muster station."

I stare at the big doors on the fronts of the drones. When those doors open, ropelike devices extend out, tightly wrap their offender into a painful-looking ball, and pull them into the belly of the drone. I've only seen that happen once—in a demonstration session held in the gymnasium when I was a small child. But once was enough though to know that I didn't want it to happen to me. I know Three felt the same way. I remember the horrified expression on her face after the demonstration.

Now, when my gaze meets Three's, I see a hint of that same horror, but this time, I don't think it is horror about what could happen to her. I think the horror is that she won't be able to retrieve her baby. And she won't be able to stay with me.

"I'll see you soon," I try to reassure her.

"Yes, very soon," she says numbly, and then she turns away and begins walking slowly with Four, back in the direction we came. I try not to think that this might be the last time I see her. But the thought creeps into my consciousness anyway, forcing tears into my eyes.

Nine takes hold of my hand. "She'll be okay." It is forbidden for him to touch me outside the privacy of our domicile, but it doesn't matter now. No one is paying any attention to us, not even the security drones.

Nine and I watch the drones follow Three and Four until they round the corner and slip out of our view. Then Nine releases my hand, and we race in the opposite direction, hoping to make it to Infant Stim, before the security drones turn us back as well.

MONDAY, JULY 4
1341

SEVEN

For the first time ever, I stand with my feet on the crumbly ground that covers my former home. I try to keep my attention on Ryan as he reviews the revised plan for our mission, but I want so badly to go down into the compound right now. I need to see my family. I need to know that they're okay.

"Let's go," Ryan finally says. "Extraction teams, move in. Security team, take your posts."

As Ten and I join the line of soldiers and warriors entering the stairwells, Ryan grabs us each by the arm. "Wait in the drone," he says. "It'll hover overhead at a safe altitude until the evacuations begin—"

I pull away from him. "I'm going into the compound," I say. "That was the original plan."

"Everything's changed now," Ryan argues. "Get back in the drone."

"And where are you going to be?" Ten asks.

"I'll be assisting with the evacuations," Ryan says, gesturing to the ground.

"We're coming with you," I say.

Ryan leans in close to us. "This entire compound could explode into a billion pieces," he says quietly. "If that happens, the only people who will survive are the ones out here."

I stare hard into his eyes, forcing back tears of frustration. "If that box blows up with my family inside it, so does my life."

Ryan's jaw clenches tight. It's the exact same expression that I saw on my dad's face when he said goodbye to me on my first Warrior Departure Day. He releases my arm and Ten's too. "Okay," he says. "Go ahead."

MONDAY, JULY 4

1345

SIX

Nine and I slink though the empty corridors that lead to Infant Stim, trying to ignore the fact that our navigators have once again begun to protest our route and are insistently instructing us to report immediately to our muster station. My heart pounds uncontrollably, frightened by the knowledge that what we are doing is dangerous, but I know that it won't rest until I have Fifty-two with me.

The door to Infant Stim is shut and, oddly, I see no movement through the translucent glass. *Could the babies already be at the muster stations?* I run my arm over the entry scanner.

"May I help you?" a pleasant female voice says through the communication system.

"I need to pick up my baby," I say.

"Pickups are not authorized at this time," the voice

245

says. "Please return during afternoon pickup hours of 1805 to 1825." The robot is acting as if this is just an ordinary day.

"Don't they know what's going on?" Nine whispers to me.

"There's a relocation happening!" I shout into the receiver. "The babies need to go to the muster stations right now!"

I hear a click in the communication system. "The infants will be transported to their muster stations presently," a female voice says in a vaguely agitated tone. She must be human. But only *robots* work at Infant Stim. "Please proceed to your muster station and your child will be reunited with you there," the woman adds. Her voice is familiar, but I can't place it.

"I'm not proceeding anywhere without my baby," I say.

"I understand," she says.

I gather my strength, readying myself to face the security drones that are now surely on their way. "You should go," I say to Nine. "I'm sure they're going to send for security—"

But then the door slides open and Miss Jeanine holds out her hand, as if she wants to scan me. I put my left forearm above hers, half-expecting her to grab it angrily and drag me away. But robots don't get angry. If she is offering to scan me like this, it could only mean one thing.

A moment later, Fifty-two arrives—carried by another caregiver robot—and my smiling baby niece is placed into my arms.

"What about the other babies?" I ask Miss Jeanine. When we arrived, it seemed the robots weren't making preparations to take them anywhere. It was as if the robots weren't even aware of the relocation.

"We're transporting them to the muster stations now," she says. Behind her, robots begin to line up, infants in their arms.

"Thank you," I say, but we don't leave just yet. Nine and I stay with the robots until we are certain that the infants are being given to their families, then we final start toward our assigned station. "I'm surprised she gave our baby to us at Infant Stim," I whisper to Nine as we walk hurriedly.

"Maybe she thought it would be easier that way. Knowing that once we had our child with us we'd probably do as we were told," he says.

That's a perfectly logical thought process. There's only one problem. "Robots don't make decisions that go against rules or protocols. At least I've never seen them do it before."

"Today isn't like any other day before," Nine says.

His statement gives me a sick feeling.

Because it's true.

MONDAY, JULY 4
1351

TEN

The soldiers ahead of us exit the stairwell into an area
of the compound that Seven and I somehow never
discovered. It looks a lot like the restricted hallways near
the drone closet—with black-walled corridors lit only by
blue lights—but the hallways here run long and straight in
each direction and there are no doorways.

We follow the soldiers around a corner and enter
another long, straight hallway. Halfway through, they round
a bend and we find ourselves in a plain white room. We
crowd inside, filling the area with about forty tightly-
packed bodies, and then the two doors slide closed.

The lights above the doors change from red to green,
and the ceiling slides open. There is movement in the floor.
Not the shaking that we once attributed to The War. This
movement is taking us upward. *We're inside an elevator.*
But this is no ordinary elevator.

Above us is another plain white room. It is nondescript but I recognize it instantly. As the platform beneath our feet snaps into position, a cold shiver runs down my back. Seven's hand grabs hold of mine and I know she recognizes this room too.

We are now standing inside the Transport Chamber.

The chamber walls deopacify and one wall retracts into the floor. For the first time in my lifetime, people exit from the Transport Chamber into the plaza.

Ryan grabs my arm. "Go to Muster Station E on the tenth floor," he says to Seven and me as he points to the nearest staircase. "Your families should be there."

"Thank you," Seven says.

Ryan's forehead is furrowed. I'm sure he's wondering if he's doing the right thing by allowing us to join him on this part of the mission. There is no doubt in my mind, though, that I need to be here. And I know that Seven needs to be here too.

"Be careful," he says to us.

"You too," I say.

Ryan heads off across the plaza, and Seven and I climb the stairs that lead to the top level of the compound. Aside from the soldiers and warriors who climb alongside us, there is no life in sight. All of the occupants of our box are gathered in their muster stations, completely unaware that their lives are about to be shattered.

The stairway ends at the tenth floor, our destination. As we enter the outermost hallways, we find the muster stations—designated by green-lit rectangular borders on the floor and alphabetical letters projected on the wall. Every station is filled with orderly rows of people.

"Ten?" I hear someone call out.

It's Three.

"What are you doing here?" she asks.

I keep my voice low, aware of all the ears that are listening. "It isn't safe here. They're going to evacuate you. You need to make sure you get out at all costs."

Her eyes turn worried, and she nods her understanding.

"Have you seen my sister?" Seven asks Three urgently.

"She went to retrieve Fifty-two from Infant Stim," Three responds.

Seven looks at Three and Four's empty arms. "Didn't you go to Infant Stim too?" she asks.

"We tried, but the security drones stopped us," Four says.

"The announcement told everyone to go directly to their muster stations," Three explains. "It said that our children would be brought to us here."

I've never known Six to willingly disobey the rules. "Why did Six go to Infant Stim?"

Seven takes a deep breath. "She did what I would do."

I'm not sure whether that is meant to be an explanation or just a statement of fact. Maybe it is both. Either way, I know where we must go.

MONDAY, JULY 4

1412

SEVEN

We are about to head downstairs to Infant Stim, when a strange alarm grips the air. The shrill tone is silenced for an instant before it is replaced by a calm, controlled female voice, "Ladies and gentlemen, our organized relocation has been suspended. Please proceed directly to your domiciles. If you have not yet been reunited with your children, for their safety, they will return to Infant Stim or School where they will remain until further notice. Once you have entered your domicile, the door must remain shut and you must not leave your domicile for any reason until you are instructed to do so."

"Something's gone wrong," Ten whispers. "There's no way we've been able to ensure that the compound is safe yet. They shouldn't be cancelling the evacuation."

Normally, there would be a contingency plan for this type of situation, but our hastily-devised new mission plan didn't cover many worst-case scenarios. There just wasn't enough time to thoroughly consider every possible development, the way we normally do.

"We should check for Six at Infant Stim," I say. "If she's not there, then we should head to her domicile."

"Agreed," Ten says.

But then, out of the corner of my eye, I see a shift in the two security drones across the way. Just a moment ago, they had seemed to ignore our presence. But now, they are heading toward us, their cameras locked in on us. "Stop, intruders," they say.

And I realize that the worst possible worst-case scenario has happened to us.

"We're being hunted," I breathe.

Security drones can manage stairs, although it is a slow process. More likely, if we proceed down the stairs, security drones on the ninth floor will be dispatched to meet us. Then we will be trapped on the staircase and taken into custody. The only way to escape is for us to vanish. And I know just the place to do so. The same place I've always gone when I wanted to disappear.

When my gaze meets Ten's, I see that he realizes it too. We race to the walkway high above the plaza garden. As the security drones travel toward us, their view will be temporarily obstructed by the decorative walls that line the plaza. I wait for my opportunity and then heave myself over the walkway railing and into the drone tunnel below. A moment later, Ten drops in beside me.

I tuck deep in the tunnel—where there's no possibility of being seen by anything terrestrial—and I huddle close to Ten. For a moment, I am back in my childhood. Hiding out with him, sheltered by these curved walls. Feeling safe from anything that could harm us. But … "What if our families are in danger?" I whisper to Ten. "We can't just stay here in the drone tunnel."

He nods. "We'll wait until the coast is clear, then we'll go find them."

We listen as the sounds of people moving through the compound grow louder and then trickle away until they are gone. Six and Nine must be back at their domicile by now and the security drones have surely moved on. We are about to check, when a blast of cold air rips though the tunnel. "That's never happened before," I say, my heart picking up speed.

The air smells strange. I start to get up, but my body is too weak. It's as if someone drained all the blood from my arteries. Heaviness drapes over me. Paralyzing me. My heart slows.

And then, everything goes black.

MONDAY, JULY 4
1419

TEN

"Seven!" I call out. It should come from my mouth as a shout, but instead it slips out in a hushed whisper.

Seven's eyes are closed and her lips parted, as if she has peacefully fallen asleep. But she would never fall asleep under these circumstances. And neither would I.

Yet, that is what is happening. I can barely keep my eyes open. Everything around me is dimming and there is nothing I can do to stop it. Even my heart seems to be giving up. Instead of rallying, it slows.

Something horrible is happening. And I can't stop it.

Because the light ... my light is going out.

This can't be how it ends.

MONDAY, JULY 4
1422

JACKIE

The wounded have all been triaged and their injuries
are being attended to. It looks like everyone who was on the
beach when the base exploded will survive. Based on the
lonely bits of metal and glass that poke up above the
water's surface as the only indication that the base was ever
there, everyone who remained inside it is certainly now
dead.

The uninjured have organized into groups and tasks
have been assigned. There is much to do right now, but
there isn't much we can do. We have very little in the way
of supplies, but perhaps we will be able to salvage
something from the remains of the compound. Debris is
beginning to wash up on the shore. Everyone has been
staying back from the shoreline, at first for safety reasons,
in case there was another explosion, but now I think no one
really wants to see what's beginning to accumulate there.

"We need to take account of the bodies of the dead," a lieutenant commander says, referencing the ocean with a nod of her head. "I need volunteers."

I volunteer. I've seen plenty of dead in my life. Not that death doesn't bother me anymore. Of course it does. But it won't scar me the way it might scar some of the others, the people who've never seen anything more than a few broken bones, cuts, and scrapes. My guess is, that's most of the people here. Even the senior officers probably haven't seen the kind of trauma that every Outsider child has witnessed before they enter adulthood. People here are rarely gravely injured. They rarely die of anything other than old age.

I won't be scarred by what I see washed up at the water's edge.

I am already scarred.

MONDAY, JULY 4

1429

SEVEN

Something is pressed hard against my face, but I can't open my eyes to see what it is. I breathe deep, hoping to get more air to my brain, to help me muster my strength. When I am finally able to force my eyelids to open, what I see fills me with terrible dread.

Twelve is holding a mask tight to my face. I want to push him away, but my arms aren't even strong enough to overcome gravity. Out of the corner of my eye, I spot Ten. My neck is too weak to turn toward him, but I can see that his eyes are closed and his body limp. Did Twelve do this to us? What is Twelve even doing here? He wasn't part of this mission. He is supposed to be mustered on the beach right now with everyone else who was evacuated from the warrior compound.

Twelve pulls the mask from my face and breathes from it. The mask is extremely old-looking. The sides are lined with dry, cracked, gray rubber. Some sort of dull translucent material forms a shield for the eyes, and a separate shield for the nose and mouth. A funnel that extends down from the bottom ends in four blackened spouts that vaguely remind me of showerheads.

As I stare at the mask, I feel my tiny shreds of strength fading. But then the mask is returned to my face and I grow stronger again. Strong enough to ask Twelve, "What are you doing?"

"Waking you up," he says, just before he returns the mask to his own face.

A few seconds later, he returns the mask to me again. "They pumped this place full of sleeping gas," he says quickly.

"Who did?" I ask him.

He shakes his head. "I have no idea."

Can I trust him? Do I have a choice?

I finally grow strong enough to push the mask from my face. "Wake Ten up too," I say.

For the next several minutes, the three of us share Twelve's mask. As soon as Ten starts to seem relatively coherent, I brief him about what's happening, at least as much of it as I understand.

"We need to get out of this compound right away," Twelve says urgently.

"And leave our families behind? Not a chance," I say.

"We'll get you out, Twelve," Ten says, "but then we're going to need to borrow your mask."

"I'm not leaving until you leave," Twelve says, looking at me.

Although I initially dismissed it as a preposterous lie invented by Twelve to inflict hurt, now I wonder once again if it is possible that what he told Ten about his feelings for me is true. Despite all those years of nasty teasing, is it possible that somewhere, deep down inside, Twelve actually loves me? While that thought sickens me, I think it may be the truth. After all, he is here trying to save our lives, risking his own in the process.

Regardless of the truth—and whether I like it or not— Twelve is now part of our team. And so we make a plan that includes the three of us. We need to shut off the sleeping gas, then we will cautiously proceed with the mission to evacuate the compound. But first, we need to leave the relative safety of our drone tunnel.

Twelve tells us that he deactivated the tenth floor security drones by disabling their power packs. Ten—who seems to trust Twelve about as little as I do—insists on going up first to make sure the security drones aren't there waiting for us. He takes a minute to clear his body of the sleep gas and then passes the mask back to me. "You're up next," he tells me, shooting a warning glance at Twelve.

Twelve nods his understanding, and Ten unsteadily

gets to his feet.

"Are you sure you're ready?" I ask him.

"I'm not at one-hundred percent," he says. "But we need to go."

I give him another few breaths on the mask and then watch him climb up over the railing.

I pass the mask to Twelve, because he's looking a bit woozy. "Where'd you get that mask?" I ask him as he breathes from it.

"It was one of my great grandmother's personal items from when she came from Up There," he says. "She always said, 'If there's ever a true emergency, get the mask.'"

"She sounds like a smart lady," I say.

He gives possibly the first sincere smile I've ever seen him make. "She was."

Twelve passes the mask up to Ten. After a moment, Ten passes it back to me. I breathe from it, trying to gather my strength. Normally, climbing up to the walkway from the drone tunnel is not a big deal for me. I could do it half-asleep. I often did in my dreams. This time though, it feels like the distance from the mouth of the tunnel to the safety of the walkway is billions of stories rather than just a few feet.

I stumble into a standing position and pass the mask to Twelve.

"Ready," I say to Ten, as I reach up to him.

Ten grabs my forearms and I grab his, locking our bodies together. As I climb, my clumsy feet slip and slide on the bumpy wall outside the drone tunnel exit, trying unsuccessfully to gain traction. I start to tremble.

"I'm not strong enough," I say.

"I've got you," Ten reassures me.

And then, I feel myself rise into the air, but I am not being pulled from above as much as I am being lifted from below. I look down and see Twelve's clasped hands under my right foot, heaving it upward. Ten uses what remains of his strength and pulls me up to him. We lie together on the floor, breathing hard, fighting to stay conscious. A moment later, Twelve hands us the mask, and Ten and I regain our vigor.

"Okay," Ten says as he passes the mask back to Twelve. "Whenever you're ready."

"Give me a second," Twelve says, the mask muffling his words.

I glance around. No security drones have come for us. Maybe Twelve told us the truth about them. Maybe he did shut them off.

Twelve stumbles to his feet and hands me the mask. "Ready," he says.

I take breaths from the mask as Ten moves back into position. "Grab hold of my arms, and I'll pull you up," he says to Twelve. "You'll need to help though. Stick your feet in the grating and climb with your legs."

"Right," Twelve says, and he reaches up to Ten.

And Ten reaches down.

But their hands never make contact.

Twelve's right foot moves backward instead of forward.

By the time I realize what is happening, it is too late for anyone to stop it. Twelve's body is already falling backward through the air. Silently plummeting toward the ground ten stories below us. Falling in slow motion, as if time is attempting to grind to a halt.

Then I hear the most horrible thud I've ever heard.

Twelve is dead, as dead as Mr. Fifty-three. There is nothing that can be done to save him. The blood from his broken body now darkens the whiteness of the plaza floor. I pass Twelve's mask to Ten. Despite the unsuitability of the air around me, I can't bear to have anything pressed to my face right now. With or without the mask, I feel as though I can hardly breathe.

Ten doesn't question the tears that fall from my eyes. I'm not sure what I would say if he did. I'm not sure why they are falling. Perhaps it is because I will never know why Twelve helped us just now. I will never know the truth.

I need to believe that Twelve's final actions were motivated by good. I need to believe that there was something good inside him all along. That it was just hidden all these years by the nastiness. I need to believe that there was good inside of Twelve. It is the only way I can move on from this moment with regret rather than relief.

MONDAY, JULY 4
1443

JACKIE

It takes a while to assemble a team to retrieve the
bodies. There are many volunteers, but the lieutenant
commander turns most of them down. I'm not sure what
criteria she used to accept me. We've only worked together
once, on the mission to gather intel after the annihilation of
the Outsider compound. I suppose the fact that I survived it
unscathed speaks to my strength, although the lieutenant
commander has no idea exactly how much.

The sixteen of us—eight robot support staff and eight
humans—travel down to the shoreline as a unit, holding
close to each other even though it makes more sense for us
to spread apart in order to more quickly accomplish the task
at hand.

We approach the first body together. Intermittent
waves wash over it. Kelp drapes it like a death shroud.
Another soldier and I step into the surf and drag the body

onto the sand.

It isn't until I release it that I allow myself to look at it.

My jaw falls open and I feel the power drain from my muscles.

What I see shocks me to the core.

MONDAY, JULY 4

1454

TEN

I press the mask to Seven's face and hold it there until her trembling hands reach up and push it away. "We need to keep going," she says.

"Right." I pull my focus from the horrible sight in the plaza garden and breathe through the mask. I'm not sure what to feel right now. I never liked Twelve. He was cruel to someone who I love. He hurt her so many times. But that doesn't change the fact that he lost his life just now while protecting hers.

Seven and I pull the weapons from our ankle holsters and head toward the control hub of the compound. At every corner, we stop and check for security drones before continuing but, as Twelve promised, there seem to be no active drones on the tenth floor.

"We can enter the control hub through the technology center," I tell Seven. It's a path I'm familiar with because of the numerous times I've visited my father at work.

We are just a few feet away from the technology center door when I steal a glance around the next corner and spot a security drone. Neither its red emergency lights nor its yellow non-emergency lights are illuminated, and its camera doesn't seem to register my presence, but I pull back quickly anyway. "There's a security drone there, but it looks inert," I say to Seven. "Cover me. I'm going to check it out."

As Seven holds her weapon ready, I round the corner and approach the drone. The thing gives no response to me at all. I make my way around the back of it and find that a rear panel has been removed. Some of the wires inside are disconnected, but not all of them. Whoever deactivated the drone clearly knew what they were doing.

"All right," I call to Seven in a hushed voice. "Come on."

Seven joins me and takes a surprised look at the disrupted innards of the drone. "You think Twelve did that?" she asks me.

"Everyone else seems to be locked in their domiciles or asleep," I say.

As I pull a security code for the technology center door, I breathe through the mask. Then Seven and I ready our weapons, and I scan open the door.

Inside the technology center, about a dozen bodies

litter the ground and chairs. The people appear uninjured and they are breathing. They're just victims of the sleeping gas, I hope. I do a quick survey of the bodies. Strangely, none of the people here are my father's technology colleagues. "They're all administrators," I say.

"What are they doing here?" Seven asks.

"They probably convene as part of the evacuation protocol," I suggest. "But if that's the case they should be in the control hub."

"Maybe they succumbed to the sleep gas before they made it that far," Seven says, and then she adds under her breath, "I wonder if they're Decision Makers."

"They could be," I say. My mom isn't among them though.

We each take a few breaths with the mask, and then I lead Seven toward the mirrored walls that encircle the control hub of the compound. My mom told me that the walls are only reflective on the outside. From the inside, they appear transparent. And so if there is anyone awake inside the control hub, they know we are coming. I scan open the door, preparing myself for whatever unknown might be inside. I prepare to fight for our lives.

As the door slides open, I find myself staring at someone who I never expected to find here, even though it makes sense for her to be here … my mother. She's wearing a mask like Twelve's, only it is much newer looking. I feel the intense urge to lower my weapon, but I don't, because in my mother's hands is a weapon exactly like ours, trained on us.

My mother is sitting all alone at an impressive workstation, with more monitors than I've ever seen in one location, except for the command center at the warrior compound. The monitors are alive with data, as well as security video images showing dozens of empty rooms and hallways here at our compound.

"What are you doing?" she asks us.

I can't respond. I've lost the ability to think coherently … to speak. My mother with a weapon trained on us doesn't make any sense at all. It is inconceivable.

"We're here to help," Seven answers for us both.

My mother's brow furrows. "Why do you have your guns pointed at me?"

"Why do you have yours pointed at us?" I force out, unsuccessful in my effort to keep my voice calm and steady.

"Because I believe our goals are different," she says.

I feel as if I've been slammed in the gut. *How could she doubt that our intentions are positive?*

"We're just trying to protect everyone," Seven says.

My mother shakes her head. "You've failed miserably at that. The Point Dume military base has been annihilated, along with your commander and the majority of his senior officers."

"We believe the commander decided to set off a self-destruct mechanism—" I start.

"He did nothing of the sort," my mother says quietly. "Every one of his actions was under my direct orders and mine alone."

"How could that be?" I ask.

"I am the Decision Maker," she says. "The only one."

My mind stumbles. Is it possible that my mother is the sole person in charge of *everything*? Responsible for all the good and the bad? Willing to exterminate those who don't suit her purposes? Willing to execute Fifty-two, and Seven, and me. *No, that can't be true.* Perhaps there were things going on that she didn't know about. My mother can't possibly be the one to blame for all that is wrong here.

"The commander was having clandestine meetings," I tell her. Surely she isn't aware of this fact. The commander made extensive attempts to hide these meetings from surveillance.

"Those meetings were about you," she says. My skin turns ice cold as her gaze shifts from me to Seven. "Both of you," she adds.

"Why were they having meetings about us?" I ask. I know many possible answers, but I need to understand her thought process, even though that seems an impossible task.

"We were attempting to determine how to control your

rebelliousness. How to use your creativity to benefit the warrior program, without allowing you to sabotage it." She sighs. "From the time you were very young, I believed that you would someday be substantial assets to the program. But now, thanks to you, it is no more."

"We didn't destroy the military compound—" I argue.

My mother holds up a hand to stop me from speaking. "*I* demolished the base," she says. "You left me no choice."

My hands shake with anger, but I maintain the aim of my weapon fixed on my mother's chest. "How could you do that?" I ask.

"If it wasn't for the warrior program, your grandparents would have been casualties of The War, and none of us would have ever been born. The warrior program helped save the world, but you were determined to compromise it."

"So you blew up the military base … and all those people?" I ask incredulous.

"Changes to our program would send a dangerous ripple through every warrior program on this planet. It is better to destroy a bad seed than to allow it to germinate and poison the entire garden," she says. "I couldn't let this program fall into the wrong hands."

"The wrong hands?" Seven asks.

She nods. "Yours."

Without a flicker of hesitation, my mother fires off two

shots. One hits my left flank. The other must hit Seven's right arm, because her weapon falls to the ground. By the time I spin around to return fire, my mother is gone.

I don't go after her. For one thing, Ryan told me never to follow an attacker under any circumstances and, for the other, on the monitor above the seat my mother occupied, there is now a clock counting down the seconds, along with words in flashing red:

DESTRUCT SEQUENCE INITIATED.
EVACUATE IMMEDIATELY.

I pass my warrior necklace to Seven. "Close the door and keep guard over it," I tell her.

My left side aching as if it has been cut from my body with a knife, I run to the monitors, grateful for a chair to sink into when I arrive there. I try to open up a menu or some means to control what is being played out on the screen, but nothing I do has any effect.

"It's locked," I say, feeling my strength fading.

Seven brings the mask to me, while keeping her weapon pointed at the door. "Keep trying," she urges me.

And then the door slides open. I aim my weapon at the doorway, certain that my mother, worried that her inept attempt to neutralize us might not have been enough, has returned to disable us completely. But instead of my mother, four masked black-jumpsuited soldiers appear in the doorway. Their raised weapons are aimed squarely at us. Did my mother send these soldiers? If so, we are now outnumbered and cornered.

"Don't shoot. We're on the same side," I say. I hope that is true. Right now, there are very few people in authority who I trust to do what is right.

"Everyone, stand down!" It's Ryan's voice.

I allow myself to exhale as weapons are lowered and Ryan files into the room, along with a half-dozen soldiers. He tosses Seven and me each a mask like the ones he and the soldiers are wearing. I put it on quickly, because I'm starting to feel lightheaded, and my full strength returns almost immediately.

"One of the administrators activated a self-destruct sequence," I tell Ryan. I can't bring myself to say that it was my mother who did this. "The system is locked out. We only have twenty-eight minutes left."

A soldier gestures to someone behind him. "We captured a female after exchanging fire with her in the passageway behind the hub."

Another soldier brings my mother forward, holding her firmly by both arms. "Is this your administrator?" he asks me.

I look my mother in the eyes, searching for regret, but I don't find it. "Yes, it is," I say.

"You think she can assist us here?" the soldier asks Ryan.

My mother shakes her head. "There's nothing I can do. Once the sequence has been activated, there's no going back."

Ryan dismisses her conclusion with a shake of his head. "Pearson, Hyde, see if you can disarm the system," he orders. Two soldiers join me at the monitors as Ryan continues, "Meanwhile, we need to clear the air and proceed with the evacuation."

Just before I turn back to the screens, Ryan leans close to my mother's ear and says in a low voice, more angry in tone than I've ever heard it, "Tell us how to turn off the gas."

MONDAY, JULY 4
1505

SEVEN

While Ten and some soldiers work on stopping the
self-destruct sequence, other soldiers occupy themselves
with the system that sends forth the sleeping gas. Ten's
mother refuses to assist them, and so the process consists of
painfully slow trial and error.

Finally, there is a reassuring onscreen confirmation:

Gas flow: zero.

Ryan places his hand on Ten's mother's shoulder and
references the bodies lying lifeless in the technology center.
"I want to see all those people out there wake up
immediately. How do we do that?"

"I don't know," Ten's mother replies coolly.

"We could try utilizing the negative pressure system,"
a soldier suggests.

"All right," Ryan agrees.

But what if that doesn't work? What if Ten and the soldiers can't stop the compound from self-destructing? What if we can't get everyone out of here in time? I have a feeling that Ten's mother could help us if she wanted to, but she's unwilling to assist us. Furious, I step toward her. The soldier who is restraining her gives me a look of warning, but I move even closer and address her anyway, "Why do you want everyone here to die? These people considered you their friend. Their family ..."

Her gaze falls to the floor. "Death is better than the alternative."

"Which is what?" I ask, even though I don't trust her to answer truthfully.

"I've already notified the other warrior programs that we have been fatally compromised," she says. "If we were to survive, we'd be entirely on our own. Like the Outsiders."

"That's better than being dead," I say.

"I disagree," she says as if it is the final word she ever hopes to utter.

I feel as if I've been trapped inside a horrible dream ... a nightmare. Never in any worst-case scenario would I have imagined that something like this would occur. People here have lived their entire lives trusting the Decision Makers to do what is right. They still trust them now. Most everyone has locked themselves inside their domicile, awaiting the Decision Makers' instructions. They don't know that there is only one Decision Maker. And that she has chosen to do the unthinkable ... She has made the decision to end all of their lives.

"Contaminant gas levels have dropped to undetectable," a soldier reports. "We can proceed with the emergency evacuation."

Through the walls of the control hub, I see the people in the technology center sitting up, looking around with confusion.

"Keep her quiet," Ryan tells the soldier guarding Ten's mother. "I'm going to make an announcement." The soldier slides a switch on the side of Ten's mother's mask, and Ryan presses a gray button on the wall and speaks, "Ladies and gentlemen, it is imperative that you proceed immediately to your muster stations and follow the instructions that will be provided to you there. Thank you for your cooperation."

I go to Ten's side. He looks away from the monitors for a split second, letting me know that he's aware of my presence.

"I'm going to make sure our families get out of here," I say to him. "Then I'll come back."

He turns toward me and locks his gaze with mine. "Don't come back," he says. "I want you to be safe."

"I want *you* to be safe too." I know that if Ten is unable to stop the compound from exploding, he won't leave. Not unless I'm here with him. "That's why I'm coming back."

Before he can argue, I race out the door.

MONDAY, JULY 4
1510

SIX

Nine scans open his personal drawer and begins frenetically tucking items into his pockets. "In case we're not returning here, I want to have my things," he says.

"Good idea," I agree.

Fifty-two lets out a soft whimper. She's probably hungry. Her last bottle was administered by the robots over three hours ago. I go to the cabinet where Fifty-two's bottles always appear in time for her feedings, just in case one has been delivered, but of course the cabinet is empty. Fifty-two is still supposed to be at Infant Stim. There is probably a bottle waiting for her there.

She looks at me with an eagerness that fills me with painful guilt.

"I'll get you something to eat as soon as I can," I tell her. "I promise."

She smiles, full of trust even though I am unworthy of

her confidence. I have no idea when her next meal will come, or even if we will survive whatever we are about to face.

"Ready?" Nine asks me.

"Almost," I say.

There is something here that Fifty-two needs. Not in the same way that she needs food, but maybe almost as much. I scan open my personal drawer and pull out the folded paper that contains Seven's letter to her baby. I also collect Jose's rook because, for some reason, the thought of having it comforts me. I slip both items into my chest pocket.

"I'm ready now," I say to Nine.

Then I scan my drawer closed.

MONDAY, JULY 4
1512

SEVEN

"Where are you going?" Ryan asks as he catches up with me in the crowded hallway.

"I need to make sure our family gets out of here." I probably should have told this to him before I left the control hub, but I didn't want him to do anything to impede me. I'm fairly certain that Ryan would like to send me out of the compound. So I am out of harm's way.

"I'm coming with you," he says, falling into step beside me.

"Why?" I ask, wary.

"I've abandoned my family far too many times in the past," he says. "I won't do it today."

I've abandoned my family many times too. I did it to protect them. Because I was forced to. To save their lives. But those facts do nothing to diminish the guilt that haunts me. I suppose a similar guilt plagues Ryan as well. "I understand," I say.

He nods. "I know you do."

As we approach Muster Station E, I hear my father exclaim, "Six! Six!" He is joined by a chorus of voices, including my mother's and Forty-one's. "Six! Six! Over here!" they call out to me. Even though my mother, father, and brother must know my true identity—based on the fact that I am wearing a black warrior jumpsuit—they keep the truth hidden.

And then my dad spots Ryan. "Seventy-two!" he says, his jaw slack with disbelief. "You came back!"

Ryan pulls his brother into a tight embrace. "I told you I would."

He did?

When I left to become a warrior, I didn't promise anyone that I would return here. I didn't think it was possible. I wonder whether it was confidence or hopefulness that led Ryan—nearly twenty years ago—to tell my dad that he would someday come home. It must have been the latter. I can't imagine that anyone who ever left our compound heading to The War ever thought they would survive to come back home.

Ten's father approaches us. "Where's Ten?" he asks me urgently.

"He's working on a critical mission," I answer. "His mother is with him. He sent me to make sure you get out of here—"

Suddenly, the wall slides open, revealing the restricted hallway beyond it. Gasps from the people around us are interrupted by a female voice from overhead, "Please proceed through the passageway, follow the lighted arrows to the staircase and climb to the top. You will be greeted there by individuals who will direct you to a safe zone."

I search the crowd, but I don't see Six or Nine or Fifty-two. "Where's my sister?" I ask.

"I haven't seen her yet," my mom says. Her statement sends my heart into my throat.

I turn to Ryan. "I have to go find my sister and the baby."

In Ryan's eyes, I see uncertainty. He can't protect everyone here. And neither can I. We must both make a choice. "I'll come with you," he says.

I can't leave the rest of my family unless I know they will be safe, and that I kept my promise to Ten to make sure his family is protected. "You need to make sure everyone else gets to the surface," I implore him. "I'll be fine."

Ryan checks his navigator. On it, I see the time count down past twenty-five minutes. He looks back into my eyes and exhales. "I want you out of this compound in twenty minutes. Are we clear on that?"

"Yes, sir," I say, but we both know that he has given me an order I can't obey. I won't leave this compound until everyone I love is safe.

As I turn away, my mom wraps me in an embrace. For a fleeting moment, I am a small child again … a child who still believes that, whenever I am in her arms, there is nothing that can hurt me. But of course that was never true. We were always in danger. And now, the danger is greater than ever.

Reluctantly, I pull myself from my mother's arms.

"I need to borrow your navigator," I say.

Without a word, she removes it from her wrist and discretely passes it to me. I clasp my hand tightly around hers as I accept it. Then I release her and watch my family and Ten's disappear with Ryan into the crowd of evacuees.

I activate the navigator and send Six a message:

It's your sister.

I'm at your muster station.

Where are you?

MONDAY, JULY 4
1515

SIX

As we climb the plaza stairs, heading to our muster station, people begin swarming the stairways. I hear urgent shouts. "The eighth floor muster doors won't open," one woman calls out as she fights her way downstairs. "We need to try a different level."

My navigator vibrates with a message from my mom … no, it's from Seven. *Seven!*

"My sister is here!" I say to Nine. "She's at our muster station."

He assesses the packed staircase above us. "It'll be a half an hour before we make it to the tenth floor."

I type into my navigator:

We're at the eighth floor.
The muster doors won't open here.
The plaza stairway is packed.

A moment later, I get a response:

I'll meet you on the eighth floor.
Muster Station E.

MONDAY, JULY 4
1517

SEVEN

I squeeze past the slowly-moving throng in the tenth floor restricted hallways and through the corrugated passageway that leads to the evacuation stairwell. I head downstairs, opposite the direction of those below me.

"You're going the wrong way," a man calls out to me. He's the father of one of my classmates.

"I need to assist someone down below," I say.

He nods and continues on his way, but as I descend, I have to dodge several others who also question my course. I wonder whether they're merely concerned about me or if they're worried that I know something they don't. The people here are surely uncertain as to what is happening, but they've been trained all of their lives not to question rules and instructions. Still, there must be a few who are wondering whether they should turn back. I know I would if I didn't know the truth.

I wish I could tell them what lies ahead, but the fact is I don't really know. And even if I did, there's no time to convince them that everything they've been told all of their lives about Up There is a lie. At this point, the only way to save their lives may be to blindly follow orders, just as they've been trained.

I bolt out of the stairwell on the eighth floor and rush through a corrugated tunnel that holds no one. It's a good sign that the tunnel is here though. It means that the compound has prepared itself for evacuations from this floor. I just hope the entrance that leads from the compound to the restricted hallways is able to function.

Up until today, I didn't know that there are restricted hallways on the periphery of any floor other than the tenth, but apparently there are such hallways on every level. The entrances to most of the restricted hallways have probably not been opened since people first arrived at this compound. Maybe not even then. I don't know if the ones on the eighth floor will open now, but I have to try. If the plaza stairways are overwhelmed, there's no way Six and Nine and Fifty-two will make it to the tenth floor in time. And many other people will not be able to evacuate either.

I follow the reverse of the route that I took just now in the tenth floor restricted hallways and find myself facing a wall. In the dim blue light, I spot a scanner. I pull Ten's warrior necklace from around my neck and scan it.

The red light on the scanner flashes. *The scanner is working. It just needs an acceptable code.* I capture a code and transfer it to Ten's necklace. Then I scan the necklace again. I am rewarded with a green light and, more importantly, the door slides open.

Standing there, looking at me wide-eyed, are Six and Nine. In Six's arms is Fifty-two. She has grown so much since I last saw her. In one heartbreaking moment, I feel the loss of all the moments of her life that I've missed. *But if this mission succeeds, I won't miss any more.* I pull the three of them into the restricted hallway. "Follow me."

Six and Nine aren't the only ones who follow. Others funnel in behind them. Together, we join the horde on the evacuation stairs, marching upward. It isn't long before we see light up above and feel the air from Outside pushing into the stairwell, urging us back down.

A woman ahead of us slows and turns to the older woman next to her. "What do you think is up there?" she asks, her voice trembling.

I am about to respond when a small voice steps in, "Don't be afraid, Mommy." A little girl, who appears no more than five years old, clutches the woman's hand. "We're going to be okay," the girl adds.

This child doesn't know what we are about to experience. Even I don't know for sure what our futures will hold. But everything inside me tells me that the little girl is right. We once lived in fear of Up There. A place that was once dangerous. A place that still is dangerous. But not in the way we were lead to believe. "We're going to be okay," I echo.

The woman cautiously continues up the stairs with her daughter and the older woman. They follow the others through the doorway and blink against the bright sunlight. Then the little girl looks up in awe at the vast blue cloudless sky. And I see her smile.

"Murphy!" Thirteen shouts. She's standing a few feet away from us, directing bewildered evacuees on where to go.

I urge Six and Nine toward her. "Go wherever Thirteen tells you. I'll meet you there," I say as I turn back toward the stairwell.

"You're not coming with us?" Six asks.

I look into her frightened eyes. "Ten is still down there," I tell her.

I haven't informed her of the imminent threat facing our compound. It wasn't safe to do so with so many other people around. I couldn't risk being overheard and inducing a panic. Perhaps it is better right now that she doesn't know.

"Go," I say.

I can tell that it takes every bit of strength that she has to turn away.

Thirteen leads Six, Nine, and Fifty-two toward a huge tent where others have already gathered, and I return to the stairwell. As I descend, I see Miss Teresa climbing up the stairs. In her arms is a frail old woman, likely too weak to make the climb on her own. Miss Teresa isn't the only robot who has come to someone's aid. Behind her are many others. Every robot is assisting a human. They are taking care of us, just as they have always done.

I suppose the robots are programmed to respond to any need for help with their assistance, even if it is outside the range of their normal duties. I once thought this type of response was specific to humans, but I now know that not all humans respond that way. I guess it depends how we are programmed.

"*Muchas gracias por todo*," I say to Miss Teresa, trying to thank her, not just for her current actions, but for everything she's ever done for us.

"*El gusto es mío*," she responds with the same words that she always gives when I thank her. But then, as we cross paths, she adds, "It is nice to see you again, Two Thousand Seven."

That is something she's never said to me before. Of course, I've never seen her outside the confines of our compound. Still, I wonder how she recognizes me without having scanned me. And even more disconcerting: how she recognizes me as who I really am. If Miss Teresa can tell me apart from my sister …

But there is no time to consider that now. There is no time to think of anything other than the most pressing issue facing us: Unless someone is able to put a stop to it, in just minutes this compound will be destroyed along with anyone who remains inside it.

I weave my way down to the tenth floor and back to the control hub. When I enter, I report directly to Ryan. "I found them. They're safe now."

"Good," he says, and then he adds, "You shouldn't have come back here."

I check the screen in front of Ten, and my heart sinks into my stomach. The clock is still ticking down. The time remaining is now under six minutes. It appears that Ten and the soldiers have made little if any progress toward shutting off the self-destruct mechanism.

Ten's mother is standing off to the side of the room with her guard. Her hands are still bound behind her back with metallic bands. She stares at the clock, her expression one of resignation. I'm not exactly sure why Ryan has kept her with us. Maybe he was hoping that she'd reveal some way of stopping the self-destruct sequence before our time ticked away. But I have a feeling that, even if there is a way of stopping it, she won't reveal it. She has already made her decision.

"It's time to move out," Ryan says. "The compound is

almost fully evacuated. The nearest exit is three minutes from here. That leaves us less than three minutes to climb the stairs and get 500 feet away."

"Hold on. Hold on," Ten says. I've never seen him look so frustrated. Of course his frustration makes sense. He doesn't want to see our home explode any more than I do, especially not at the hands of his own mother.

"Our families are waiting for us up there," I say to him gently.

He shakes his head. "I need more time."

"We don't have any more time," I say.

"Please—" Ten starts.

Ryan grabs his arm. "HANSON, WE NEED TO GO NOW!"

Ten resists for only a moment before all of the fight drains out of him. He points at the monitor. The fight goes out of Ryan as he stares at the screen. Ten's mother moves closer, her guard in tow.

And then I see what has captivated every eye in the room, and sucked out all the sound, and the air, and the breaths.

"That's impossible," Ten's mother says. "It couldn't be done."

But it has been. On the screen, the numbers on the clock have frozen, as if time itself has stopped. Above the clock is a new message:

DESTRUCT SEQUENCE TERMINATED.

Ryan's face fills with relief so strong it almost looks like pain. He puts his arm around Ten and starts to lift him to his feet, but Ten pulls away.

"Hold on," he tells Ryan.

I watch as he brings up a file. And the computer asks:

Are you sure you want to permanently delete
DESTRUCT_SEQUENCE_FILE.EXE?

Ten selects "yes."

A moment later there is a confirmation:

DESTRUCT_SEQUENCE_FILE.EXE PERMANENTLY
DELETED.

Ten's mother shakes her head. Forbidden tears fill her eyes.

I take Ten's hand and hold it tight. Clinging to what is still good. The battle is over. But no one has won. Our lives have been changed in a way we never anticipated. We have learned the ultimate truth. A truth that was as painful to discover as it was necessary to know.

And now we must move forward. We must attempt to

put together the pieces of our shattered existence … and our broken hearts.

MONDAY, JULY 4
1528

SIX

Nine, Thirteen, and Four have gone off in search of infant formula, and my parents have taken Forty-one to try to find a lavatory in this barren place of far-away buildings and even-farther-away walls, leaving Three and me alone at the periphery of the evacuation area with our babies. We sit close together on a dark-green sheet that has been set on the ground. The conversation of the hundreds around us is muted. Some people seem to be in shock, sitting entirely still as their gaze darts this way and that, probably utterly overwhelmed by the thoughts in their brains. The only people who seem unaffected by the situation are the youngest of the children.

"Are you scared?" Three finally asks me.

Her question makes sense. Fear of the unknown used to trouble me, sending me into a state of panic. Right now, any reasonable person would be absolutely terrified. But strangely … "I'm not."

"How can you not be scared?" she asks.

"I think it's because we're together," I say.

"You think we'll have to stay up here?" she asks, her eyes anxious.

"Whether we stay up here or not, everything has changed." There must have been a very powerful reason behind this evacuation. There had to be. Now one of the biggest secrets of our existence has been exposed. Now everyone has seen what is above the sky. I can't even imagine where our lives will go from here.

Three takes a shaky breath and leans close to me. "I love you," she whispers.

And everything stops. All I see and hear and feel is Three. She has never said those words to me, even though I've known them to be true ever since the moment we met. I am about to respond when I feel a hand on my shoulder. I turn and see Seven and Ten. They sit down beside us, appearing exhausted. They seem unwilling to speak, maybe even unable.

Before I ask any questions, Nine, Thirteen, and Four return, along with Nineteen. Thirteen passes two very small baby bottles to Three and me. The labels say "Dextrose water."

"Sugar water?" I ask.

"It's the only thing we could get," Thirteen says. "The nurse said it would keep the babies hydrated and healthy until they can bring in fresh supplies."

"The infant formula in the evacuation kits expired years ago and it was never replaced," Nine adds. "I don't think they ever really planned on evacuating our compound."

"You're probably right." I uncap the bottle of sugar water and offer it to Fifty-two.

"Twelve is dead," Seven says.

"What happened?" Thirteen asks with a gasp.

"He fell," she says. "During the evacuation of our compound."

Twelve mercilessly abused Seven from the time we were young, and I despised him for it. Still, I never wished him dead. I don't think she did either.

"What was he doing here?" Nineteen asks. "He wasn't supposed to be on this operation."

"I think he followed me," Seven says.

"Why would he follow you?" Four asks, perplexed.

"To protect me," Seven says quietly. "He saved Ten and me today, losing his own life in the process."

Four's brow furrows. "What would possess him to do that?"

Seven inhales. "He did it because he loved me."

MONDAY, JULY 4
1534

SEVEN

I don't give anyone time to react to my revelation. I don't want to hear any debate. There is nothing that would convince me that my statement isn't true. *Twelve loved me.* I will let him leave the legacy of having died while protecting someone who he cared about. The same way I would have done had I died today.

I don't tell them that we *all* nearly died today. That Ten's mother tried to kill us all. And I won't. That truth will likely be disclosed to everyone in time. Holding back that information harms no one. Ten's mother has been taken away. She can't hurt us anymore.

I push on, "They're going to move everyone into temporary housing until the safety of the underground compound can be confirmed. They'll start transporting people soon. Ten and I are going to head out on one of the aerial drones. There's room for all of you, if you like."

"I'm going to stay and help out here," Thirteen says.

Nine steals a glance at her and she smiles shyly at him. "I'd like to stay too," he says.

Nineteen and Four decide to stay as well. Six and Three choose to join us. Before we go, Nine lightly touches Fifty-two's forehead. I wish I could find the words to express my gratitude for what he has done for my family. But even if I could, I don't think I have the strength right now to make them come without tears. And so I just offer him an embrace.

Ten, Six, Three, and I collect my parents and brother and Ten's father and sister and bring them to the waiting aerial drone. We tell them that Ten's mother must stay here, a fact that keeps hidden the larger truth, at least for now.

Once we're all settled into our seats, with our harnesses fastened, and with Fifty-two in my arms and Fifty-one in Three's, the drone lifts up into the sky. My brother struggles to spin around in his seat in order to look out the window. He's so small that the harness gives just enough to allow him to do it. Ten's sister spins around as well. Her mouth falls open as she takes in the view of the myriad treetops and tiny houses far below us. In the distance, the dark shimmering ocean meets the pristine blue sky.

"This place looks like a fairy story," she says. "Is it real?"

My words catch in my throat. It takes a moment before

I can answer her.

"It isn't a fairy story," I finally say. "*This* is above the sky."

MONDAY, JULY 4

1544

JACKIE

Once we've collected the bodies that washed up from the ocean, the lieutenant commander tells everyone on the team to take a break. I walk far down the beach, away from everyone else, beyond the barrier constructed to hide the remains of the dead.

I remove my tablet from my pocket to check for messages from my people. I haven't given up on the five who survived the initial wave of destruction, and I won't until I have proof of their deaths. Perhaps now that things have changed here, I can convince the military to send out search drones. If the survivors are out there somewhere, maybe we can find them …

In the inbox, I see something that makes my heart nearly leap from my chest.

There is one new message. From this morning.

My entire body is trembling by the time I get the first word decoded.

I keep translating letter by letter:

> We are at the rally point.
> Limited food and water supplies.
> Communication is spotty.
> Can you hear me?
> Jose Alvarez

Could it be true? Could Jose still be alive? And he said "we." That means others are still with him. They need help. But I can't help them alone.

I activate my navigator and send a message to Ryan. Words that I hope will cause the same response in him that they do in me:

> Jose Alvarez is alive.

MONDAY, JULY 4

1549

SIX

I chose a seat between Ryan and Three. Ryan, because he was with me the last time I found myself flying in a drone, high in this infinite sky; he protected me the last time I was up here. And Three, because being next to her always makes me feel better.

Sitting on the other side of Three is a woman who looks to be about the age of my parents. Strangely, she is wearing a white jumpsuit. I've never seen someone so old wear a white jumpsuit. The woman's gaze meets mine and she smiles.

"My name is Maria," she says to me.

"I'm Seven." I lie because, as much as I wish I could be honest now, I'm still not sure it's safe to reveal my true identity. Especially to strangers.

"You look so much like your sister," she says.

"How do you know my sister?" I ask, hoping for a clue as to the woman's identity.

"I was once a warrior," she says. "Years ago, I was captured by a group of people referred to as Outsiders. They imprisoned Ryan and your sister. I was involved in their escape from captivity."

And then I realize, *Maria doesn't know my sister, she knows me.* I must have met her during my time up here, the part of time that was wiped from my memory.

"How did you help them escape?" I ask.

"I was just a small part of it really," she says. "Most of the plan was crafted by my son, Jose. He nearly died in the effort."

It takes all of my self-control not to gasp. *This woman is Jose's mother.* And she said that Jose almost died during my escape from the Outsiders. Could that be true?

"Is Jose here?" I ask, trying not to let my eyes search the faces of those inside the drone. I shouldn't be looking for Jose because I would not be expected to recognize him.

"No," she says. "He's back home at our compound."

"I'd like to meet him," I say.

Maria's forehead creases. "You would?"

"Yes ... well ... he saved my sister's life."

Ryan reaches across me and touches Maria's arm. "I need to talk to you right now," he says to her. His tone is serious, reserved. Not what I would expect given that, if Maria has told me the truth, she is responsible for both him and me surviving our imprisonment.

Ryan turns to me. "Would you mind switching seats with her?"

He helps me release my harness, and Maria and I trade places. I try not to listen in on their conversation, because it isn't polite to do so, but I can't help overhearing Ryan's first words. And they make my heart freeze: "Jose needs help."

"What's going on?" Maria asks him.

"Apparently he's about ten miles away from the site of your old compound. At some sort of rally point. It's not in a secure area and he doesn't have much water—"

"What is he doing there?" she asks, sounding worried.

Ryan exhales. "There's something I need to tell you," he says gently. "Just after they extracted you and the other former warriors from the Outsider compound, the entire community was leveled by the military."

Maria's eyes search the empty air, as if looking for something to hold onto. "What about all the people who lived there?" she asks Ryan.

"Up until just now, I didn't know there were any survivors," he says. "But apparently there were five."

"Only *five* people survived?" she whispers.

"You have to help them, Ryan," I blurt out.

"*Seven*," Ryan says, no doubt trying to remind me who I am supposed to be. "This doesn't involve you."

I stare into his eyes. "Maria told me that Jose is

responsible for saving the lives of you and my sister. If that's true, we must try to help save his." It isn't until the words come out of my mouth that I consider them. These words didn't come from my brain, they came from my heart.

"Don't worry," Ryan says. "I'm planning to do everything in my power to help Jose."

"You are?" Maria asks, sounding surprised.

"Of course, I am," he says. "I owe that boy my life."

"I want to help," I tell him. Although these words don't sound like something I would ever say under such obviously dangerous circumstances, they are true.

Until recently, the thought of coming back up here made me feel as if I was going to pass out from panic. But now, it is the thought of inaction that makes anxiety rise in my chest. I wonder if that's how Seven felt one year ago when I sobbed and told her of my incapacity to be a warrior. Maybe that is what forced her to act. The need to do what is right rather than what is safe.

I once believed that Seven and I were only alike on the outside. But maybe I'm more like my sister than I thought. Or maybe I *can be*. Maybe I can be courageous rather than cowardly. Brave rather than afraid. Strong rather than weak. For the first time, I feel ready to find out.

MONDAY, JULY 4

1623

JACKIE

The drone carrying Ryan, Murphy, Maria, and the others lands far off on the beach, in order not to disturb the numerous work sites we've set up here: first aid stations, a makeshift hospital, rest stations, salvage stations, a morgue, among others. I run to the drone and help people debark: Murphy and Ten, two middle-aged men, a middle-aged woman and a young woman, two children, and two infants. Some of the soldiers debark as well. Then I board.

Left inside the drone are Ryan and Maria, along with about a dozen soldiers. Strangely, a girl who must be Murphy's sister remains onboard. She looks so much like Murphy that, had I not seen Murphy debark just moments ago, I would think it was her. This girl, though, wears a navy-blue jumpsuit, like the other adults who we are leaving on the beach.

"Davis, this is Seven," Ryan says to me. "She's Murphy's twin."

I give her a quick smile and she smiles back appearing tense. *Even her smile is familiar.*

"It's nice to meet you," I tell her.

She nods. "Same here."

Ryan offers me the empty seat next to him. As I adjust my harness, he asks, "How confident are you in your intel about the Outsiders?"

My heart speeds. *I can't disclose the source of my information without exposing my identity.* "I'm extremely confident," I tell him, and then I hesitate, afraid to say anything more. If I reveal the reason that I know Jose is in danger, I risk everything, but then again, everyone on this drone has volunteered to help my people. They are willing to head into danger based on the information that I've provided. I take a deep breath and admit, "I received a direct message from Jose." And then I add, "He sent it to me because ... I'm an Outsider."

"That's true," Maria confirms to Ryan. I suppose that means she agrees with my divulging this secret. Perhaps it is safe to do so now. The military leaders who would have destroyed me are dead.

Ryan shakes his head in disbelief. "You're a spy?"

I nod, feeling the shame of betraying his trust.

There is more that I should say. Eventually, I must tell Ryan that I supplied the intelligence that led to his and Murphy's imprisonment by my people. And that the intelligence I provided led to the ambush that killed his wife. I will tell him all this, but I can't risk telling him now. Right now, I must make him understand why I did it. This mission depends on it. All it would take for the mission to be instantly abandoned is Ryan's word.

"I infiltrated into the military because our people were dying of injuries and illnesses that are easily treatable," I say, desperate for him to understand. "And they needed water to drink that wouldn't make them sick. The military had so much excess that they were disposing of expired supplies every day. All we wanted was *their trash*. To save our people's lives. The military refused to give it, so we were trying to take it. If your mother or father or brother or friend was suffering, wouldn't you have done the same thing?"

Ryan looks at me for a moment before he exhales. "Show me what you've got."

I open my tablet and bring up Jose's messages. "I received the first one a week ago. It lists the names of the five who survived."

"May I see?" Maria asks.

I pass the tablet to her and watch her read each name:

Selena Brown
Tamara Brown
Kris Chang

Andrew Fishman

Jose Alvarez

Maria passes back the tablet and closes her eyes. "My little babies are gone."

I knew Maria's youngest children well. Katrina was eight years old. Stacy was four. And little Noah was just two. Of Maria's children, only Jose survived. The anguish that contorts Maria's face and turns it to an awful shade of red is something I've seen on the faces of too many parents. I can't imagine the agony of being unable to protect my children from death.

"It isn't right," Maria whispers to Ryan.

"It isn't," he says.

Grief darkens his face as he folds her crumpled body into his arms.

MONDAY, JULY 4
1642

SIX

We've just been given an ETA of five minutes when one of the soldiers—who had been looking out of a drone window through a long binocular device—calls out, "We've got about twenty Outsiders traipsing through the field here. Any chance these are friendlies?"

Jackie leaps from her seat and peers through the device. "I don't recognize them," she says. "They're not from our tribe."

The soldier returns his focus to his device. "Well, these guys are heavily armed and they appear to be en route to our destination."

"I'll knock them out with the stunner," another soldier says.

"Negative," Ryan says. "We can drop a pulse shield, but we'll need to go in fast on the extraction."

"With a pulse shield, we only have fifteen minutes," a soldier argues.

"And you don't think we can retrieve five civilians in fifteen minutes?" Ryan asks.

The soldier stares hard into Ryan's eyes. "I think it's not worth the risk."

"Look," Ryan says. "We're on this mission to save lives. Too many were lost already. If we stun those Outsiders in the field, thirty percent will never wake up. Wait until we're ready to descend, and then drop the shield."

The soldier looks back to the window. "Copy," he says. "Ready the pulse shield to drop when we reach our target coordinates."

"That's the right thing to do," I say quietly to Ryan. "You don't know if those people are our enemies."

"In this world, everyone is your enemy until they've proven to be your friend," he says.

Before I can consider his statement, the pilot calls out, "We're at target coordinates."

"Drop the shield," Ryan says. "Be ready to move."

In an instant, everything outside of the area immediately below us disappears into shimmering clouds. It is as if energy from the sky descended to the ground, leaving only the tube-like path in which we travel untouched. This path must lead to the spot where Jose is waiting.

Ryan grabs my wrist. "When we land, you stay in the

drone," he says to me.

Reluctantly, I nod. I know that outside the drone I'd be more of a hindrance than a help. I have no military training other than that given to me by Ryan in the little white room in the Outsider compound. A room that is no more because the military destroyed it.

The military destroyed everything. That must be what they do. Or at least what they used to do. Now it appears that they are doing just the opposite. The people in this drone are risking their lives to save the Outsiders.

The drone sets itself down on the brown lumpy ground and soldiers pour out of it, along with Ryan and Jackie. Maria and I are left inside, along with a few soldiers who, based on their continued activity with various devices, seem to have important jobs to do. One of the soldiers calls Maria over to help him with some task, leaving me all alone.

I wish I had a job right now, something … anything … to distract me. But I don't. And so I sit and wait, hoping that within the next fifteen minutes I'll see Jose again. Alive. Knowing that if I don't, I probably never will.

MONDAY, JULY 4
1649

JACKIE

I've been to the rally point only twice in my life. The last time was seven years ago. Trees and bushes have grown up over the mouth of the cave, even more than the last time I saw it. The other soldiers and I quietly slice away the dense shrubbery. It doesn't matter that it will take years for it to hide the opening of the cave once again because, after we rescue Jose and the others, this rally point will have completed its service. There is no one left in our tribe to need it.

Once there is enough of an opening in the foliage, we release an aerial surveillance drone. Inside the face shield of my helmet, I see video of the dirt-caked rock walls of the cave from the drone's point of view. The first portion of the cave is empty, and so we begin to enter. We don't have much time. The pulse shield begins to dissipate soon after it is dropped. By fifteen minutes, it can be penetrated by weapons, and those Outsiders who we saw heading in this direction will certainly be waiting to engage with us.

My helmet provides me with vision in the darkness, but all I see around me are the same rocky cave walls that the drone showed us moments ago. Of course I wasn't expecting a welcoming committee. Jose and the others should be safely ensconced deep within the cave. There is a large cavern inside that is stocked with emergency supplies. It is a convoluted path to the cavern, with multiple branches. It would take hours to search all of them and we have only minutes. I hope I remember the way.

Suddenly, the drone footage goes dead.

"What happened to the surveillance feed?" Ryan asks, his voice transmitted directly into our helmets.

An answer comes from one of the soldiers who we left inside our aerial drone, "The readout indicates a malfunction in the surveillance drone."

"Do we have another one?" Ryan asks.

"Negative," the soldier says. "We weren't properly supplied for this mission and—"

"Right. Okay," Ryan says. "We're going to proceed. Everyone be ready to engage with whatever is in here. The people we're here to rescue might not see us as friendly."

I feel my body tense. Already our mission has taken a turn in the wrong direction.

Ryan leads us forward until we come to a fork. "Which way?" he asks me.

"Left," I say.

And so we go left.

The cave is narrower here. Only about four people wide. We travel as a unit. The soldiers at the rear watch our backs, just in case. Suddenly, two shadowy figures appear around the bend ahead, and then quickly retreat from view.

"Two on the left!" Ryan growls. "Take cover!"

It's unlikely that anyone other than my people is in here, but we can't take any chances. I press my body up against the cave wall and then call out in the direction of the figures, "It's Stephanie Cortez!" I use my real name— my Outsider name—to identify myself to my people. "We're here to help!" I add. I sent Jose a text message letting him know we were coming, but I don't know whether he received it. Last I checked, I hadn't received a reply.

In the silence that follows, two weapons peek around the bend.

And, in that same instant, two soldiers beside me fall to the ground.

They shot at us! Why did they shoot at us?

We return fire, spraying the air ahead even though the attackers are no longer visible.

A distant voice pierces through the battle. "There are eight more of them heading at you!" The voice is Jose's.

And so, the firefight we've engaged in isn't a mere

misunderstanding. These attackers are our enemies. And there are at least eight additional enemies inside the cave who are heading toward us. Add them to the two we've already seen, and that makes at least ten attackers. And only six of us are still able to fight.

A large man peers around the cave wall and promptly drops, along with another soldier behind me. I blast the darkness with energy. Whoever is out there must be stopped. We have only minutes before we'll need to retreat. We need to end this now.

On Ryan's order, we push our way forward. Another attacker drops. Then another. Near one of the lifeless bodies, I see the crushed remains of our aerial surveillance drone. It has been damaged beyond repair, and the trauma to the little drone doesn't appear accidental. Our attackers must have destroyed it and then positioned themselves to destroy us.

At the limits of my visibility, I see no one else ahead, but there are certainly more enemies. At least seven more. And we're down to five soldiers. Ryan is lying on the ground. Unconscious.

Right now, there is nothing I can do to help Ryan and the others. More attackers are coming and our time is fading. We need to incapacitate our assailants, retrieve Jose and the other survivors, and get the hell out of here. Retreating now would mean leaving Ryan and the other wounded soldiers behind, as well as Jose and the surviving Outsiders. That is something I will not do.

We advance quickly, checking around each corner for potential attackers, me deciding our route because I am the only one who might know the way through this maze. I want to call out to Jose, but to do so would reveal our location to enemies who may not be able to see in the dark as well as we can.

And then, up ahead, I see five large men coming at us with weapons drawn, shooting as they run, as if they have nothing to lose. My only protection is my weapon and those of my fellow soldiers. And so I fire. And fire.

And I watch the attackers fall. One. Two. Three. Four. Five.

And then it is silent. And we're down to four soldiers still standing.

If Jose's information was correct, there are at least two more attackers.

I see movement in the dimness ahead. I aim my weapon, but then I see what's there.

"EVERYONE, STAND DOWN!" I shout. "She's one of us."

About twenty feet away is Maria's oldest daughter, little Katrina Alvarez. Very much alive. In her hand is a small flashlight. She wears a muddied nightgown that's torn away along the bottom. Her little arms and legs are marked with scabs and bruises, along with fresh blood. The dirt masking her face is streaked with tears.

"Are there any bad people with you?" I ask her, keeping my gun raised.

She shakes her head. "All of the grownups are dead."

"Come here," I tell her. "Run."

As she arrives, I pull her into my arms. She isn't trembling or shaking the way a small child should be under these circumstances.

"Where's everyone else?" I ask her.

"In the big room," she says.

"Show us where they are," I say. "Quick."

I stay close to Katrina as she runs through the passageways, ready to protect her in case there are threats ahead. The other soldiers keep pace with us. And then Katrina slows. We all do. The sight ahead would make anyone pause.

Bodies litter the ground. The bodies of my people. Deathly still. I run to Jose's and put my hand on his chest. Tears of relief surge to my eyes as I feel movement.

"He's breathing!" I call out to the other soldiers.

I hear replies of "This is one too" and "This one's breathing." The soldiers quickly secure the wrists and ankles of the unconscious. I understand why. They can trust no one. I leave Jose unshackled though. It isn't necessary to restrain him. I trust Jose with my life.

One of the soldiers checks on the only adult female survivor, Selena Brown, who lies near a wall, her body partially hidden by broken boxes of supplies. Her breathing is shallow, but she has a strong pulse in her neck. Nearby, are the bodies of two hulking strangers who are either unconscious or dead. A soldier secures the wrists and ankles of the one who is unconscious. The other man is dead.

I speak into my communicator, "The threat appears to be neutralized. We have four of our team down. Four unconscious friendlies. Ten hostiles down as well. We're going to need assistance getting our people out of here." *And we don't have much time.*

"Jose's not dead?" Katrina asks me.

I wrap my arms around her, wishing I could have protected her from the trauma of what she must have witnessed here but, even at her young age, she has probably seen much worse. "Jose is sleeping," I tell her. "We're going to take care of him while he tries to wake up."

I glance at the chaotic remnants of supplies scattered throughout the cavern and see no signs of life other than my fellow soldiers, who are tending to the unconscious.

According to Jose's list of survivors, Selena's baby daughter was among them. The child must be here among the rocks and ruins. But if the infant was stunned, the odds of her survival are poor. Children don't tolerate stunning like adults do. One stun in a vital area is nearly one-hundred percent fatal in little ones.

"Katrina," I say gently. "Is there anyone else?"

Slowly, she nods.

MONDAY, JULY 4
1658

SIX

It has been almost ten minutes since Ryan, Jackie, and the other soldiers disappeared into the hole in the mountain. About three minutes ago, more soldiers left our drone, heading into the hole. No one has told me what's going on, but I've overheard enough to know that what is happening in there isn't good.

"They're coming out!" one of the soldiers onboard our drone shouts.

I'm not sure how she knows this. I see no activity at the edge of the hole.

And then I do. Soldiers begin appearing from behind the trees and bushes. They are dragging something with them. *Bodies.*

Horror fills my chest as body after body is dragged or carried toward our drone. The formerly-controlled space around me becomes a flurry of activity. Maria and I dive toward the door. Ready to help care for the wounded.

Medical equipment appears. Helmets are removed, and oxygen masks are strapped onto the faces of the casualties.

A body is deposited on the floor at my feet.

"Ryan!" I shout even though he is clearly deeply unconscious.

"Is he injured or stunned?" Maria asks one of the soldiers.

"Stunned, we think," the soldier replies before running back out of the drone, I assume to retrieve more victims.

Maria and I carefully remove Ryan's helmet and someone hands me an oxygen mask. Numbly, I strap it to Ryan's face. Attached to the mask, there is a bag which inflates with air.

"If he stops breathing, squeeze the bag once every five seconds," a soldier tells me. And then she moves on to the next victim.

For a moment, I am alone in The White Room with an unconscious Ryan. Screaming at him. Panicked and desperate. Begging him to wake up.

The only thing that snaps me back to the present is the arrival of another body.

Jose's.

Another oxygen mask is placed into my hands. Automatically, I strap the mask over Jose's mouth and nose. And then my hand takes hold of his so easily that it seems strange. Oddly, I have no qualms about touching him. He feels familiar to me, like my family, and Nine, and Three. It feels right to touch him, to comfort him. But I don't think Jose is aware of my touch. Even though his fingers are warm and pink, and I feel the steady throbbing of the pulse in his wrist, when I lift his eyelids, his eyes are fixed far away.

Suddenly, I hear a scream. It isn't like the fearful screams I've made in the past. Or the screams of joy I've heard from delighted children at family recreation. It is the scream of a child though. A scream of relief and pain wrapped into one sound. And then there's a word, "Mommy!"

I look up and see a little girl, about six or seven years old, running into Maria's open arms. At the drone doorway is Jackie, with a bright-eyed but scruffy-looking young child on each hip—one boy and one girl.

Maria scoops up the oldest girl and embraces the two younger children as she cries the same two words over and over, "My babies! My babies! My babies!"

Moments later, the drone door is shut and we lift off into the sky. The shield around us must be gone now, because the monitors are registering weapon hits on our drone and the soldiers are arguing about how we should retaliate. I keep my focus on Ryan and Jose.

I squeeze Jose's breathing bag. He is no longer breathing on his own. Maria watches me work as she clutches her three small children in her arms. Her face remains stoic and free of tears as she listens to the oldest girl recount what happened to her people.

"After they stole you away, the bad guys came with smashers and tried to kill everyone," the girl says. "But Noah and Stacy and me hid in the tunnels. When the smashers went away, we went to the rally spot, just like you and Daddy always told us. And then more bad guys came, and Jose told us to hide … Then Jackie came …"

My mind doesn't follow what the little girl is saying, because it stopped at her very first words. I stare down at the unconscious faces of Ryan and Jose, and I hear the girl's words repeat in my head, *the bad guys came with smashers and tried to kill everyone.* Those "bad guys" were the military. The same military who took our warriors from us every year. Seven, Ten, and Ryan were all part of the military. Did they participate in something so awful as destroying children?

This question haunts my brain. There is only one person here who I trust to answer it, and he is unconscious. Ryan skips a breath, and I squeeze the bag attached to his mask, forcing his lungs to fill with air. Hoping that he'll wake up.

Please, Ryan. Please wake up.

MONDAY, JULY 4
1702

SEVEN

When we arrived on the beach, we were each given a
brief medical exam in the triage area. Fifty-two and Fifty-
one were provided with a few ounces of oral rehydration
solution along with a promise that baby formula will be
included in the shipment of food and water that is expected
to arrive from a nearby compound within the next hour.

After we've all been released from triage, Ten and I
walk down the beach with our families and Three, and we
find calm spot to rest. The adults settle on the sand,
cautiously exploring it with their fingers, intermittently
glancing at the remarkable sights around them before
retreating their gazes to the soothing, comforting ground.
Forty-one and Forty-seven quietly toss around a basketball
that one of the soldiers found for them. Their minds seem
far away. Perhaps they are contemplating their new
surroundings, where the basketball is the only thing that is
familiar.

We've been resting for only a minute or so when Twenty-two approaches. "Hanson, Murphy," he says, still using our warrior names. "I need to speak with you."

I pass Fifty-two to my mom, and Ten and I get to our feet.

Twenty-two leads us away before he speaks again, "Prior to departing for her mission, Lieutenant Jackie Davis told me there was something I should show you."

He directs us past a barricade, and I am immediately struck by the horror of the scene before me. Laid out on the beach in neat rows are bodies—or, more correctly, the shattered remains of bodies. None are intact. All that is left are torn fragments of bone, muscle, and innards. It's difficult to believe that what I see here were once parts of living, breathing people.

"The commander is over there," Twenty-two says, pointing to a large bloody lump a few feet away. "Using DNA, they were able to identify remains from everyone who was supposed to be in Conference Room 24."

And so those who perished when the military compound exploded weren't robots. The commander, Carter, and the others who were locked inside the conference room were human, like us. But, in a way, they weren't like us. Their minds didn't function like ours. These people were willing to destroy rather than protect. To hurt rather than heal—

"Why did Lieutenant Davis want us to see this?" Ten asks.

"She didn't say," Twenty-two replies.

As I stare at all that is left of the people who once commanded us, I come up with an answer to Ten's question. It's just a theory, but it's the best one I have.

"Can you give us a moment?" I ask Twenty-two.

"Of course," he says.

I wait until he is past the barricade before I say, "I think Jackie wanted us to see what we did to them."

Ten shakes his head. "We didn't do this."

"Indirectly, we did," I say. "We set a chain of events in motion. This wasn't our intention, but it was the result."

His expression clouds and he looks out toward the ocean, toward the scene of the destruction of the place we once thought of as our second home. "Had you known the outcome, would you have still agreed to this mission?" he asks me.

My answer is complicated. As a result of our mission, my friends and family are now safer than they were before. But people died today. The warrior compound was demolished. And Ten lost the mother he thought he knew …

"I would never intentionally destroy someone or something good," I say. "But I would have proceeded with our mission, even if I knew this would be the result."

"Me too," he whispers.

Tears blur my eyes as Ten takes me into his arms. It feels comforting to be close to him again. In his arms, my sadness lessens even though nothing about our lives has changed. Sometimes, like right now, I wish I could hold onto Ten forever, and never face the daunting future.

Our embrace is interrupted by Twenty-two, who comes running past the barricade, calling out, "Ryan and Davis are incoming!"

Ten and I follow him to the landing site as an aerial drone descends from the sky.

"Stay back!" a soldier orders. "Maintain a clear a path to emergency triage!"

"Who's hurt?" I yell, but no one answers.

The drone doors burst open and soldiers carry wounded from the aerial drone. Some of the injured wear tattered clothes and others wear jumpsuits. And then I see Ryan. Lifeless. Carried by two soldiers. The top of his jumpsuit has been opened and monitoring probes have been attached to his chest. A medical resuscitation mask covers his mouth and nose.

"Ryan!" I shout, running toward him.

Soldiers make half-hearted attempts to push me back, but I make it to Six, who is by Ryan's side, squeezing the bag attached to his mask every few seconds. "What happened to him?" I ask her.

"They think he was stunned," she says. "We'll have to scan him to make sure."

I shake my head, feeling painfully helpless. "We don't have a scanner here. We hardly have anything."

The soldiers place Ryan on a clean white sheet on the sand and doctors and nurses begin to work on him. Listening to his chest and abdomen. Checking his pupils. Reviewing the readouts from his monitors. "Give us some room," a nurse tells me.

I move back, but I keep watch as Ryan is cared for with the limited tools we have. Six continues to assist him with each breath, gently squeezing the resuscitation bag ...

A hand falls onto my shoulder. *Jackie's.*

"What went wrong?" I ask her.

"We were ambushed by another tribe of Outsiders," she says.

"Are you okay?" I ask, looking her over.

"I'm not injured," she says, and then she adds, "but there's something I need to tell you."

My mind swims with the possible horrors she might share. "What is it?" I force myself to ask.

Jackie inhales deeply before she quietly says, "I'm an Outsider."

"What?" I ask, certain that I've misheard her.

"The people we retrieved just now are part of my tribe," she says.

"Did Ryan know?" I ask, still trying to make sense of her confession.

"I told everyone who was on the mission. They deserved to have that information before they put themselves at risk." Her tone tells me that she has more yet to say.

"Why are you telling me?" I ask.

"My tribe was the one that attacked your terrestrial drone nine months ago and then your aerial drone a few days later. Both attacks were based on information that I supplied."

"You helped the Outsiders ambush us?" Pain and anger burn my chest. "My instructor died because of you."

She lowers her head. "We were trying to take warriors hostage. We were hoping that you might be sympathetic to our cause. That, if we told you the truth …"

I move toward Jackie, wanting to destroy her. A person who I once trusted. A person who betrayed me. But I don't do anything to her. Because no matter what I do. I can't change the past.

"I'm so very sorry, Murphy," Jackie says. And then she turns and walks away.

MONDAY, JULY 4
1820

SIX

Over the past hour, I've watched the nurses care for Ryan and Jose. Medicines have been administered. Tests have been performed. But no one has told me the results. The doctors and nurses are focused on saving lives. That's where I want their focus to be. And so I just sit quietly. Keeping vigil.

Someone kneels beside me in the sand, so close to me that I know instantly who it is.

"Three," I whisper, then I look at her.

Her eyes are red from crying. "I was worried about you," she says.

"I'm sorry I left on that mission," I say. "But I had to …"

"I understand," she says. But how could she possibly understand? I never told her about my time with the Outsiders. With Jose.

He lies on the sheet to my left, not moving other than

the slow rise and fall of his chest with each breath. I gesture to him. "That's Jose," I say to Three, keeping my voice low.

"He helped you escape from the Outsiders," she says, repeating what Maria told us.

"I don't remember him doing that, but I know deep inside that it's true," I say. "If it wasn't for Jose, I don't think I would have ever made it back home. I think ... I *know* ... Jose saved my life."

"What makes you so sure?" she asks.

"Jose was kind to me," I say. "He was gentle and caring ..."

Her brow furrows. "How do you know that? I thought they wiped your memory."

"They did," I say. "But only some of it. I remember the first few months I spent up here."

Her eyes widen. "What do you remember?" she asks.

"Jose and I became very close," I admit.

"Did you love him?" she asks, her voice unsteady.

I need to be honest with her. "I think I did."

Three looks at me, her eyes uncertain.

"But not the same way I love you," I breathe.

"You love me," she says quietly, half-statement, half-question.

"Yes. I love you," I say. "I wanted to tell you that earlier today. When you said it to me. I've been meaning to say it for so long—"

Three's gaze shifts to Jose's bed.

I turn and see that Jose's eyes are tentatively starting to open. I look back to Three. "I need to go to him," I say.

"I know." She gives me a small reassuring smile. "Go ahead."

Surreptitiously, I take her hand and squeeze it tight, hoping that it will act as the embrace we both need, but don't dare carry out. Then I close the distance between Jose and me.

"Murphy," he says, unfocused, maybe still half in a dream. After a few moments, his gaze finally centers on my face and he smiles. "I heard you were coming to help us, but I didn't dare to believe it," he says and then he exhales, as if he is disappointed. "You don't remember me. They wiped your memory."

I can't respond properly to that. It's too dangerous with so many people nearby who could overhear. I'm not supposed to have ever met Jose, because I'm not supposed to be "Murphy." I'm supposed to be her twin sister. And Murphy is supposed to have had all of her memories of Jose wiped away. Neither of us should know this boy. But of course, I do.

I won't lie to Jose. Instead, I will tell him the truth in a way that only he will understand. I unzip the chest pocket of my jumpsuit and retrieve the little white rook that I found on my nightstand in the hospital when I awoke after my partial memory wipe. I press the rook into Jose's hand, and relief washes over his face. Then he passes it back to me.

"I want you to keep it," he says.

"Why?" I ask.

"I meant it to be a good luck charm."

I've never heard that phrase before. "A good luck charm?" I ask.

He looks into my eyes. "It's a *castle*," he says. "To keep you safe."

When I was young, I used to dream of living in a castle. I believed that, in a castle, the walls would never shake, and The War could never hurt me. In a castle, I would be safe. Until recently, I never told anyone about my fantasy. I was too embarrassed to do so, because it made me sound fearful. But, for some reason, I told Jose.

I move closer to him, so no one overhears what I am about to say. "Why did you help me escape from the Outsiders?"

He doesn't take even a moment to consider his response. "The world is broken. It probably always will be, but it's better with you in it."

There is so much that I don't remember about my time with Jose. And I never will. Maybe someday Jose and Ryan will fill me in on what happened during those months that I can't recall. But I already know for certain that Jose's kindness, his caring, our friendship ... it was all real. And my biggest question about Jose has now been answered.

Jose saved my life because he cared about me enough to lose me forever.

MONDAY, JULY 4
1855

SEVEN

Fifty-two is asleep in Ten's arms, after finally having received her bottle of formula. My parents and Ten's father sit quietly with Maria and Three, who has Fifty-one asleep on her shoulder. With exhausted eyes, we watch Forty-one and Forty-seven build a castle out of the sand with Maria's young children—Katrina, Stacy, and Noah. In Maria's arms is the infant of an Outsider woman who is still in the medical area, along with Ryan. Six has been providing us with periodic updates on Ryan's progress. Last we heard, he was still unconscious.

Suddenly, Six comes running down the beach, heading toward us.

"Ryan's awake!" she calls out. "The nurse said he can have two visitors at a time."

Maria and I jump to our feet. As we start toward the hospital, I allow Maria to get a bit ahead of us, then I turn to Six. There's something I need to make sure she knows.

For her safety. "Did Jackie tell you that she's an Outsider?" I ask her.

She nods. "She told us right before the mission."

I can't help feeling a bit surprised. "Did she tell you that she was responsible for the Outsiders capturing you and Ryan?" I ask.

Six's eyes narrow. "She was trying to save her people," she finally says.

"Her people could have killed you," I counter.

"Like our military killed them?"

My gut twists. Because Six is right.

"The war isn't over," she says quietly. "As long as people are in danger, they will fight to protect themselves and their loved ones."

Just as I did today.

I mustn't blame Jackie for fighting to protect those she loved.

There is only one right thing to do here.

I must forgive her.

MONDAY, JULY 4
1901

SIX

When Seven and I arrive at Ryan's bedside, Maria already has him wrapped in an awkward embrace, one arm around him, the other cradling the infant we recovered from the Outsiders' cave. When the two separate, Ryan looks at the child in Maria's arms.

"Whose baby is that?" he asks.

"Her mother is Selena Brown," Maria says. "You *met* Selena during your time with us."

Most people wouldn't catch the veiled meaning of her statement, but I understand it instantly. Ryan must have been forced to mate with Selena while we were held captive by the Outsiders. I see in Ryan's eyes that he understands Maria's inference as well.

"I remember Selena," he says. "She seemed sad. More so than the other women."

Maria nods. "Her husband died years ago. She said she'd never love anyone else. She wouldn't even look at another man …"

"Is she here?" Ryan asks, glancing around.

I answer before Maria can, because she is unaware of the information that I have, "Selena's heart stopped." I let them follow my gaze to her body, about ten feet away, wrapped up tightly in a white sheet, the way dead bodies are. I continue, "The doctors and nurses tried everything they could, but they weren't able to revive her." I can't help thinking that, had we been back home, with all the medical equipment and scanners at our disposal, the outcome might have been different.

Ryan reaches toward the baby's tiny hand, touching it ever so lightly, and I see his eyes fill tears. They might be tears of sadness, but mixed in with them, I know there's the love of a father for his child. A child he always wanted, although certainly not under these circumstances.

As Seven and I move away to give Ryan some privacy, I look toward Jose's bed. He's sitting up on his sheet, appearing surprisingly well aside from the monitor probes still affixed to his chest. I direct Seven toward him.

"That's Jose," I tell her.

"You must be Murphy's sister," he says to Seven as we approach. "She told me a lot about you."

I don't remember telling Jose much about Seven but, with all the time we spent together, I must have.

"It's nice to meet you," Seven says.

"Same here." Jose gives her a smile and then looks back to me. "I thought it might be hard to tell you two apart, but it isn't difficult at all."

He could be joking, but based on the look in his eyes, I suspect he's being truthful. I suppose I should be worried. If Jose can tell us apart, it won't be long before he realizes the truth about our identities. And it may be a while before it's safe to reveal our switch to everyone.

But I feel certain that Jose can be trusted.

How can I not trust the boy who gave me a castle to keep me safe?

MONDAY, JULY 4
1955

SEVEN

It takes nearly ten minutes of searching before I spot Jackie organizing the supplies that have been pulled from the ocean. The others working with her are robots. As I approach, Jackie steps away from me, concerned perhaps that I have come to attack her.

"Can I help?" I ask her.

Her eyes search mine for a moment before she says, "The usable materials go to the right. Everything else to the left."

I head for the collection of debris near the water and pull out large broken piece of a monitor. Unusable. I bring it to the left. Jackie and I meet up again at the pile of rubble. "I want to apologize for my anger earlier," I say.

"It's understandable. Your instructor was an innocent victim." She drags a crate of intact dishes from the pile. I help her to haul it to the right, until a robot comes over, lifts the crate, and carries it off to the pile of serviceable items.

"I know you never intended to hurt her," I say as Jackie and I return to the debris pile.

"Anna was a good woman." She grabs an unidentifiable gray hunk of plastic and starts off rapidly to the left.

I snatch up a broken wheel and shattered bucket and follow her. "I'm sorry about what happened to your people," I say.

She dumps her load without looking at me. "Go be with your family, Murphy."

"Why don't you join us?" I offer.

She waves her hand dismissively as she heads back toward the ocean. "I'm okay on my own."

I step in front of her, forcing her to stop or go around me. She stops. And then I notice that her eyes are wet with tears.

"I know you are," I say. "But I'd like you to join us … if you want to."

She gives a hesitant nod. "All right."

MONDAY, JULY 4

2002

TEN

The kids have finished constructing a large castle made of sand, almost as tall as Maria's little boy. They fill the moat with ocean water, using salvaged drinking cups. It's slow going because the cups are small and the moat they've excavated is wide and deep. This seems like a good time to speak with my father, and so I lead him away, close enough that we can keep an eye on Forty-seven, but far enough that no one overhear us.

I decide to get right to the point. "The military took Mom into custody."

Strangely, the tension in his body relaxes a bit. He almost appears relieved.

"She told me that she was the Decision Maker," I continue. "She said she was the only one. Is that true?"

He swallows. "Yes," he says. "That is correct."

"How long have you known?" I ask him.

"She informed me shortly after you were born," he

says.

I exhale, a bit disappointed that he knew all this time but never told me. Then again, I'm sure my mother never would have allowed him to do so.

"Did she talk to you about her decisions?" I ask.

He looks out at the horizon, where the setting sun has turned the sky crimson. "Only once," he says. "When she decided to send you up here. I think it was her most difficult decision."

"Did she tell you what it was really like up here?" I ask.

"She said only that you would be safe," he says.

"But what about The War?" I argue.

"She said you'd be protected."

"Then what was she concerned about?" I ask, although I'm not sure whether he has any idea of the answer.

"She wanted to send both you and Seven, but she thought it was best that the two of you be separated ..." he starts.

My heart pounds with anger that is only held at bay by the sleeping baby in my arms. "Why?" I ask.

"She feared that together you were dangerous."

It turns out that her fears were well-founded. We *were* dangerous. To her.

"Did you agree with her?" I ask.

He shakes his head. "She wasn't interested in my

opinion. I think she was primarily trying to convince herself that sending you up here was the right decision. She loved you, Ten. She didn't want to let you go."

I take an enraged breath. "She tried to kill me today," I say. "She tried to kill all of us."

My father's eyes fill with horror. "What did she do?" he asks.

I point at the remains of the warrior compound that protrude from the turbulent ocean. "She destroyed the compound where the warriors lived. There were numerous casualties. Then she tried to obliterate the compound back home with everyone still inside it."

His gaze falls to the sand. "A few months after you left, your mother changed dramatically. She seemed troubled, and she wouldn't tell me what was wrong. I thought it was because she'd lost you."

"That wasn't it," I say. "She was worried about Seven and me damaging her precious warrior program."

"Her grandfather established that program," he says. At first I think he is offering an excuse, but perhaps it is meant as an explanation. He continues, "He was the very first Decision Maker. Before he died, he told us that he hoped you would follow in his footsteps. Unfortunately, your mother went against his wishes."

Suddenly, I understand the reason behind all the time my great grandfather and I spent together. He was teaching me to be the Decision Maker. *That* is why he spent countless hours showing me how to access forbidden files. *That* is why he gave me the cellular and the chips that offered me the freedom to explore. *That* is why he taught me not to be afraid to use my brain to question things. To think for myself. To do what I thought was right.

Today, my mother tried to destroy us.

But my great grandfather gave me the tools to stop her.

MONDAY, JULY 4
2024

SEVEN

Not long after Jackie and I settle down with my
parents, Ten rejoins us with his father and Fifty-two. Ten
appears a bit calmer now. I assume he told his father what
happened in the control hub. Perhaps his father found
words to reassure him. I hope that I too will find them
tonight when we are alone together.

In the darkening ocean, shadowy ships emerge to carry
us to the abandoned military facility in Santa Monica, our
temporary new home, where we will reunite with those who
once shared our box under the ground and start the process
of rebuilding.

I suppose eventually our box will be ready for
rehabitation, and people will go back down into it and live
out the rest of their days hidden in the ground. But, their
lives will be different. Because now they know the truth
about Up There. A truth that, up until just hours ago, was
forbidden to even consider. Now, it is impossible *not* to

consider it.

Now everyone knows that Up There is a place full of possibility. A place not unlike a fairy tale. Where forests and animals and oceans actually exist. A scary, magnificent, beautiful place.

For now, we will *all* live in that place.

For the first time in our lives, we will all live above the sky.

About the author

J.W. Lynne has been an avid reader practically since birth and now writes inventive novels with twists, turns, and surprises. In the science fiction series THE SKY (ABOVE THE SKY, RETURN TO THE SKY, PART OF THE SKY, and BEYOND THE SKY), an eighteen-year-old fights to survive in a dystopian future society founded on lies. The romantic contemporary novels LOST IN LOS ANGELES and LOST IN TOKYO follow a young woman's journey after a horrible betrayal. KID DOCS dives into the behind-the-scenes action at a hospital where children are trained to become pint-sized doctors. In WILD ANIMAL SCHOOL, a teen spends an unforgettable summer working with elephants, tigers, bears, leopards, and lions at an exotic animal ranch.

55343639R00215

Made in the USA
Middletown, DE
16 July 2019